I0825459

WILD JUSTICE

Center Point
Large Print

WILD JUSTICE

Alan LeMay

CENTER POINT LARGE PRINT
THORNDIKE, MAINE

This Center Point Large Print edition
is published in the year 2026 by arrangement with
Golden West Inc.

The text of this Large Print edition is unabridged.
In other aspects, this book may vary
from the original edition.
Printed in the United States of America
on permanent paper sourced using
environmentally responsible foresting methods.
Set in 16-point Times New Roman type.

ISBN: 979-8-90082-024-8

The Library of Congress has cataloged this record
under Library of Congress Control Number: 2026935570

CHAPTER ONE

This was the crisis—the climax of all that long war. Here they sat, these men who had fought a common enemy for so long: Dusty King, who with the hoofs of countless cattle, had carved many a Great Plains trail deep into the short grass; young Bill Roper, who had begun following those trails with Dusty King before he was big enough to hold a horse; and old Lew Gordon, Texas man, whose wild marketless herds had been the roots of fortune.

Bill Roper got up to stand looking out into the night. Through the open window was coming the smell of spring on the northern plains—a wet, living odor of melted snow and new grass. It brought something keen and enlivening into the room, cutting the smoke of hand-rolled cigarettes. It was as if the night itself knew that history was being made here, among the clutter of worn saddles and ropes in this little shack on the edge of Ogallala.

Dusty King and Lew Gordon constituted King-Gordon, the famous partnership that had developed with the great cattle trails; until now, their many brands marked far-scattered herds beyond estimate. They were here because of tomorrow's auction of land leases. Under the hammer would go the grazing rights on the Crying Wolf Indian lands—those miles and miles of stirrup-deep grass that King-Gordon wanted, and that Ben Thorpe had to have.

It was curious that their long war with Ben Thorpe should have met its true climax here; more natural that it should have come in the roar and smoke of six-guns in a dusty street, or in some titanic clash in the cattle market, in which one huge organization or the other would have to go down. But the three in this room understood that the outcome would rest upon what the two older men decided here. Possession of the Crying Wolf meant dominance in the north to King-Gordon, or to Ben Thorpe—there was no longer going to be room for both.

The loose-hung frame of Dusty King slouched at rest, and his blue eyes, that never seemed to grow any older, remained noncommittal. But behind his leathery face—tough and dark from the whip of sun and sleet, and deep-carved with humorous lines—these other two who knew him could see the curious gleam that spoke of war, and delight in war.

He said, "Lew—we're looking down his throat!"

Lew Gordon sat perfectly motionless, solidly braced in his heavy chair, and seemed planted there for all time. His kind and steady gray eyes, his calm, grave face, showed him for exactly what he was—a sane, thoughtful man, in search always of the ways of security, or orderliness, of peace. He remained silent, waiting his partner out.

"This is an old fight, Lew," Dusty King said. "It goes back as far as that first time you backed me with a little herd, to see if I could make it through to Abilene. It's as old as Jesse Chisholm's wagon tracks that marked the trail I took. Don't hardly seem like we better draw back now."

Lew Gordon stirred, swaying his shoulders imperceptibly, like a stubborn bear. "Credit's going to be terrible hard, this coming year," he said at last.

Dusty King seemed to sprawl a little more loosely, playing poker in a way of his own. Swaggering, easygoing, spendthrift—he still was a man who believed invincibly in himself. He had always been in the forefront of those tough, game, Texan trail drivers who had shown the way to the others, over and over, making new trails to meet the westward-crawling railhead.

"I passed Ben Thorpe in the road today," he said. "He was looking mighty prosperous. I bet he weighs two hundred and twenty-five pounds now, with his stomach pulled in. But it seemed like he had the look of a man who knows where he's going—and how he's going to get there, too."

"His backing is terrible strong," Lew Gordon said, his eyes on the floor.

No one knew better than Lew Gordon that Dusty King, in tackling the impossible a hundred times, had a hundred times shown the way for the rest. But Gordon remembered, too, the poverty of the cattle-poor days before any outlet was found for Texas beef. To risk all they had won, in a single slashing stroke at an old enemy, was almost more than Gordon could bear.

"You know why Ben Thorpe's strong," Dusty King said. "And you know how he got his start. Folks say now that nobody knows who the trail raiders were in the cross timbers, or how come so many Texas men left their bones beside the old Sedalia trail. But you know, and I know, I think."

"Nobody could ever prove it on him," Lew Gordon said.

"Just the same, we know. And we know how he went on from there. We know why it is that so many Texas outfits stand in Ben Thorpe's name, and how many different ways he's found to jump down on little lonely Texan cowmen and leave them broke or dead. And we know what's happened to many a little trail-drive outfit that started north, but never brought their cattle through, nor got home."

Lew Gordon stirred again, but he didn't speak. Silence clamped down again in that little saddle-cluttered room, and behind it the distant bawling of held cattle made a restive background.

"Every year," Dusty King said, "since we began

driving up the big trails, we've locked horns in one way or another with this one gang. I'm not forgetting who started the Red Crick stampede where Dave and Bob Henry died under piled up cattle; nor the Tularosa shootings, with four more of my boys dead; nor the adobe ruins where old Dan Murphy's little outfit used to stand. There's some good cowboys under the prairie, Lew."

Gordon said almost inaudibly, "Never could prove anything."

"His herds have grown faster than ours have grown," Dusty King's expressionless voice droned on. "He's as big as we are, but he'll be bigger soon. From the Big Bend to the Tetons, he owns more outfits than he knows the names of. He's never run an honest deal where he could run a crooked one, nor a square trick where he could play a mean one. It's a long time since he rode all night with his rifle in his hands, but by God, Lew, if he isn't stopped—there's plenty he can hire to do his dark-of-the-moon stuff now."

"Dusty," Lew Gordon said, "we've blocked him every way we could."

"That's why he'll get you and me, too, in the end."

Again, the silence closed, with behind it the perpetual bawling of the cattle, far off in the spring night.

Dusty King said casually, "Cleve Tanner's here."

Bill Roper saw Lew Gordon's eyes flick up to look at Dusty King. "Cleve Tanner?"

"Here in Ogallala."

"What the devil's the meaning of that?"

"Cleve and Walk Lasham are the only two of Ben Thorpe's men that raided the cross timbers with him in the old days, the only two he can really trust, now."

"It's natural that Walk Lasham should be here," Lew Gordon conceded, "but Cleve Tanner, all the way up from the Big Bend—"

"Shows you," Dusty King said, "what store they set on the Crying Wolf lands. Ben Thorpe is sold mighty deep into next year's deliveries. Already he's committed for more northern-fed cattle than he can show—unless he can get the Crying Wolf."

Slowly, Lew Gordon got a frayed tally book out of his back pocket and put on a pair of gold-rimmed glasses. They looked out of place on Gordon's weathered face. Nobody knew whether those glasses did Lew Gordon any good or not. Certainly, every figure in the tally was already clear in his head. But when the time came for slow deliberation, Lew Gordon always got out the glasses and the book. Dusty King watched ironically and let him alone. Here was the old story—Gordon always thinking of the defense, Dusty King always head-up for the attack.

"The survey—" Lew Gordon's voice was curiously bewildered—"it's hard to believe there's any land as good as this."

Their private survey had been made by Bill Roper. It represented weeks of hard riding and shrewd calculation of the strength and depth of the feed upon the surface of the broken land.

"Mr. Gordon," Bill Roper said, "I've been over every mile of—"

Dusty King said, "Sit down, kid."

"One place here reads fifty head to the section," Lew said wonderingly. "Fifty head of cattle grazing one section of land! It's past belief."

"This isn't Texas, Lew."

They were silent again, waiting to hear what Lew Gordon would decide.

"I figure we might pay as high as thirty cents to the acre," Gordon said, "by the year's lease."

A flicker like that of heat lightning showed for a moment behind Dusty King's eyes, but his voice was low and monotonous as before. "Thirty cents be damned," he said.

Lew Gordon looked at him for a long time. "How deep you figure to go?"

"Get the land," Dusty King said.

"Ben Thorpe is liable to go crazy and bid his head off."

"We're looking down his throat," King said for the second time. "The least the deputy commissioner can accept is drafts on Kansas City. Ben Thorpe hasn't realized the value of the land. We'll catch him short and force him off the board."

"At what cost to ourselves?" Gordon demanded.

"At all costs."

Slowly, Lew Gordon shook his head. "Maybe thirty-five cents an acre."

Dusty King's voice rose explosively for the first time. "Thirty-five cents," he echoed—"or fifty cents, or seventy-five, or a dollar! Get the land!"

Lew Gordon stared at Dusty King for a long time. For a few moments, it seemed to Roper that a curious gleam had come up behind Gordon's eyes, but as he watched, he saw it die. He saw Gordon blow out his breath and settle his eyes stubbornly on the floor once more. He knew, as Gordon opened his mouth, what the old Texan would say.

But Dusty King cut in as Gordon was about to speak. "I'm thinking about the boys that are dead," he reminded his partner.

"It won't help them if we break ourselves now."

"I'm thinking of something else," King said. "I'm thinking of a river crossing on the old Sedalia trail. I'm thinking of a dead Negro cook, spread out on his back in the brush. And I'm thinking of a dead white man, face down in the ashes of his wagon. I'm thinking—I'm thinking of a pinto horse."

Looking at the two older men, Bill Roper

knew that something queer was happening here under the spring night. The future of a range was at its turn, but behind that, something else was changing, hidden. It was past him, then, to know what it was. Dusty King's face was smiling a little, but his eyes had turned to sleepy, tilted slits, so that what was behind them could not be seen.

Lew Gordon sighed, and he looked like a man who was weary and old. His big hands, gnarled by the years of rope and rein, dangled slack from the arms of his chair.

"You want that land," Gordon said, "even if—"

"At all costs," Dusty King said again.

Gordon looked his partner in the eyes.

"Go in and bid!"

CHAPTER TWO

Swinging down the boardwalks of Ogallala in the cool spring sunlight, Dusty King and Bill Roper looked a whole lot alike. The more than twenty years difference in their ages had not changed Dusty King's loose-jointed swagger, the rakish cock of his old soft hat, nor the cracking ring of the spurs he was believed to sleep in. The trail years had leathered his face, but they could not diminish his gay exuberance, just as prosperity was unable to take from him the look of the trail. Whatever Dusty King wore, he always appeared to be wearing disreputable saddle clothes.

Perhaps young Bill Roper had picked up a lot of Dusty King's characteristics in the course of an association that had lasted almost as long as Bill Roper's life. Literally raised a cattle driver by Dusty King, Bill Roper, too, bore the marks of the trail, so that the two men seemed to have been cast in the same mold.

Everybody who knew King-Gordon at all knew the story of Bill Roper and Dusty King. Fifteen years ago, at the age of five, Bill Roper had been found hiding in the brush, like a little rabbit, beside a wrecked outfit on the old trail to Sedalia. It was Dusty King who had found him there, and it was Dusty King who had buried the bullet-shattered body of Bill's father beside that Godforsaken trail.

In the fifteen years since then, Bill Roper had learned guns and horses and cattle, and the tricks of the trail as only Dusty King knew them. He had been able to read prairie signs before he could read print, and if it had not been for tomato can labels, perhaps he would never have learned to read print at all. Everything he knew he had learned from Dusty King. There was every reason that he should have grown to look something like the great trail driver who had brought him up.

Now, as they made their way down the muddy street, before the false-fronted wooden buildings, half the cowmen that thronged Ogallala hailed Dusty with comradeship and delight, so that his progress was that of a celebrated character, already famous. The other half—they were Ben Thorpe men—seemed not to see him at all. It was hard to tell which tickled Dusty King more—the warmth of his many friends, or the bitterness of his innumerable enemies.

The bidding for the Crying Wolf lands was being held in a disused store, and here the sidewalk and half the street were filled with knotted groups. Through this crowd, Dusty King and Bill Roper waded, Dusty trying to look like something bewildered, from the tall country. Beside the door was posted a handbill in black type, giving due legal notice of the auction of leases, and Dusty stopped to study this with a grave, empty face, as if he had never heard of it before.

"Mr. King," somebody said, "they've been waiting for you, fully an hour."

Dusty looked blank. Then he clutched his hat to his head in a startled way and rushed inside with a clownish representation of haste.

Within, the crowd of plains-country men—bronzed men, saddle-faced men, sometimes bearded men—gave way as King, followed by Bill Roper, shouldered his way to the back.

"Is this the place," King asked, "where the feller is selling the horse?"

The deputy commissioner took his feet off his table. "The sale was supposed to start at two o'clock," he complained.

A little tribute, there. The commissioner—perhaps already in Ben Thorpe's pay—hardly dared start an important sale without the presence of this slouching, nondescript-looking representative of King-Gordon.

"No word has come from your partner at all," the commissioner said.

"He ain't coming."

Three men who sat in chairs grouped around one end of the table looked at each other. They ignored King and Roper, as hostile dogs ignore an enemy of whom they are not yet keenly aware.

The big man in the light-colored hat was Ben Thorpe—*the* Ben Thorpe, whose far-scattered holdings perhaps already exceeded those of King-Gordon. Ben Thorpe, who, some thought, first learned his tactics with Quantrell's guerrillas, and got his start with those same tactics in the dark, ugly days of the cross timbers. As he sat here today, he was no longer the lean night rider, the watchful raider he once had been. Thick-shouldered now, heavy-bodied, he was today more than ever a power feared in the cattle country—still unscrupulous, still menacing, but now of a different sort—a power of wealth, of organization, and of bought-up law.

Thorpe's face was big and mask-like, with eyes heavy-lidded, sleepy-looking. The black suit he wore was well-cut, both collar and shirt freshly starched. Only the thickness of the skin of his face, laid now in rounded folds, attested his saddle years. He had a way of speaking softly, of moving softly, with a deceptive inertia.

Beside him, the tall man, lean and narrow-bodied as a slat, was Cleve Tanner: a hawk-faced man, keen-eyed, so cleanly-shaven that the tight skin of his jaw seemed to shine. Cleve Tanner was manager of Ben Thorpe's Texas holdings, the breeding grounds from which Thorpe's whole organization drew its strength.

The other, the man who seemed uncommonly dark, even among these sun-darkened men, was Walk Lasham. Some thought Walk Lasham had more than a little Indian blood, but his exact origin was unknown. Those who thought they knew all about it claimed that Walk Lasham, like Cleve Tanner, had ridden with Ben Thorpe in the bloody days of the cross timbers. He was Ben Thorpe's manager in the north, now. Under his poker-faced watchfulness lay Ben Thorpe's northern holdings, the feeding grounds now necessary for any wide operation in the cattle trade.

"Seems like," said Ben Thorpe, "we've waited long enough."

The deputy commissioner said, "If Mr. Gordon isn't coming, I suppose we might as well begin." He raised his voice. "This," he said, "is a federal auction, to place by public bidding certain lands in the charge of the Indian Department, by the authority of the Secretary of the Interior and the President of the United States, namely certain lands . . ."

He droned through his preamble perfunctorily; everyone in the crowd knew exactly what was involved. Something more than land was here changing hands. To hold the Crying Wolf would all but mean supremacy in the north. But this thing was bigger than that. The two organizations that clashed here again were the great powers of the trails. Behind each of them were whole counties of Texas mesquite grass plains, great areas of the middle short-grass country, scores of outfits. The struggle between them had developed with the Chisholm trail itself—a decade-long combat between men of diametrically opposed principles and methods. And now—

"This land," the deputy commissioner concluded, "is thrown into blocks. I think, gentlemen, you are already familiar with the placement of the lands. Block 1 includes, as previously agreed, an estimated one hundred sections, or sixty-four thousand acres, known hereinafter as 'Block T' bounded on the north by—"

Cleve Tanner leaned close to Ben Thorpe, whispered, and Thorpe nodded.

"I shouldn't think," said the deputy commissioner, "we need to hear any bid of less than ten cents per year, per acre."

"I'll take an acre and a half," said King.

Thorpe and his two lieutenants looked impatient. "Two bits an acre," said Thorpe.

"I'm bid twenty-five cents per year per acre on the hundred sections of Block 1," the deputy commissioner translated.

"On the whole sixty-four acres?" Dusty asked.

"Sixty-four thousand," said the commissioner testily.

"Mr. King, if you will please—"

"Oh," said King.

"If there are no other bids—"

"A dollar an acre," said Dusty King.

There was an instant of silence, then a stir ran over the whole packed room, rising rapidly to a hubbub as men asked their neighbors if they had rightly heard.

Ben Thorpe jerked straight up in his chair. "What damned foolishness is this?"

"You intend that bid?" the commissioner asked of King.

"I made my bid, and I'll back my bid," Dusty told him.

The deputy commissioner looked at Ben Thorpe, who exchanged a quick glance with each of his lieutenants. "A dollar, five," Ben Thorpe said.

"A dollar and a half," said Dusty King.

A red light showed for a minute behind Thorpe's eyes. "A dollar, fifty-five," he said, and settled back in his chair.

The room was so quiet now that the men who crowded it could be heard to breathe. The deputy commissioner was looking at Dusty King, and those few seconds of silence seemed to draw on and on. Bill Roper's face was mask-like. By the private survey Roper himself had made, Block 1 was broken, worthless land.

"Well, Mr. King—?" the deputy commissioner said at last.

"Who? Me?" said King.

"Do you wish to make a further bid?"

"Why, no."

There was a moment more of silence while everybody stared at him, and in that quiet, King took out a piece of twist tobacco and bit himself off a chew. With this packed in his cheek, he let his gaze rest on Ben Thorpe mildly, pityingly.

Someone in the front rank of the crowd snickered, and in another moment a rumble of laughter swept all over that crowd. These men knew what was happening here. In the few words that had been spoken, there had passed bluff and counter-bluff. More than a hundred thousand dollars had changed hands—and Thorpe had paid a record-breaking price for a vast block of land which he could put to little use.

Ben Thorpe's eyes became sleepier, his face less expressive, as the deputy commissioner spoke the ritual that gave him his hard-bid land. On the forefront of the commissioner's bald head, a faint sheen of perspiration showed.

"Open for bids on Block 2, an estimated one hundred sections, or sixty-four thousand acres, bounded on the north by—"

"Ten cents," said Thorpe, low-toned.

"Dollar and a half," said King.

Once more through all that packed room ran a curious stir, followed by the mumble of low voices. Ben Thorpe had been slowly turning his light-colored hat in his hands, but now he jerked forward and slammed it on the table with a wallop that nearly blew away the commissioner's stacks of forms.

"This is irresponsible damned foolishness,"

he said, his voice hard and clear for the first time. "By God, I'm not here to take part in an entertainment!"

"Mr. King," said the deputy commissioner, "did I understand you to offer one-fifty an acre?"

"Seems like I did," King said.

"He can't back that bid, and he knows he can't," Thorpe declared. "My understanding is that the bidder must show sight drafts on Omaha or Kansas City."

"Well, I got 'em," King said.

The deputy commissioner started to say, "I don't see how I can—"

"That's not a legitimate bid on the land in question, and you know it," Thorpe laid down the law. "All this man is trying to do is to checkerboard the Crying Wolf in such a way that it will be useless to all concerned."

There was a moment's silence, and the deputy commissioner got out a big silk handkerchief and mopped his head, as King now let a slow smile come to the surface of his impassive face. A curious rumble ran over the room, and the crowd seemed to sway.

"I got a proposition," Dusty King said. "Nobody is bidding on this land but us two; nobody means to bid. You got five blocks there. Tear up your papers on Block 1, tear up my bid on Block *2*. Throw the whole thing in one pot, and we'll bid on the works."

"I'll agree to that," Thorpe decided. The black anger in his face had submerged again, so that he was poker-eyed.

The deputy commissioner was beginning to look like a man who wished he were someplace else. "If there are no objections—" He glanced at Thorpe and began slowly tearing his previous notations into strips. "Bidding is open on five blocks of the Crying Wolf as a whole," he said, a faint, hard tremor in his voice. "Five hundred sections, or approximately three hundred and twenty thousand acres of land, bounded on the north—"

"Fifty cents," said Dusty King.

Ben Thorpe's face had turned a curious color, not gray, certainly not bloodless, but rather an odd, congested color, like dark sand. "Fifty-five," he said.

"Sixty."

"Sixty-five."

"A dollar," said Dusty King.

"A dollar, five."

"Just in confidence between you and me," Dusty King said, "Mr. Thorpe can't pay that."

Thorpe laced him with a curious, unreadable glance. "I think my name is good anywhere in the cow country," he said to the commissioner.

"It ain't good here," said King. "You just throwed it up to us, we got to show either Kansas City or Omaha sight drafts."

"God knows, Mr. Thorpe," the commissioner began, "I—"

He stopped, and with hands not altogether steady, rearranged the papers on the table, his inkwell, his pen. Sidelong, his badgered eyes drifted to Ben Thorpe's face.

They saw Thorpe nod, the faintest inclination of the head.

The deputy commissioner slapped his pen down on the table. "Gentlemen," he said, "I'm sorry to do this, but in the interests of the government, and of the Indian Department which I represent—" He hesitated, and the tip of his tongue ran along his lips.

"Spit it out," King said.

"All further bids in this auction will be accepted only as representing American gold."

"Cash on the nail?" King asked.

"Immediate payment in Ogallala." There was no question now about the sweat that stood out on the commissioner's forehead.

"Seventy cents," said King.

"I'm already bid a dollar, five!"

"Sure, but we got different rules now. God knows Thorpe can't back a dollar, five in gold. What the hell kind of shenanigan is this, anyway?"

The eyes of the deputy commissioner went to Ben Thorpe's face again, but there was nothing to be read there. Thorpe seemed so lumpishly still that it was not apparent that he breathed.

"Seventy cents," said Dusty King again in the silence. "Whoop 'er up, boys—I've only begun!"

There was silence again through the pack of those saddle-faced men, perspiring silence on the part of the deputy commissioner, and dead lumpish silence on the part of Ben Thorpe. Cleve Tanner, his hands locked behind his neck, looked at the ceiling. Walk Lasham sat motionless, his eyes on the face of his boss.

"You—" the deputy commissioner wavered, "you—you can back this bid in gold?"

"Immediate delivery by Wells Fargo," King said. "Right now, in Ogallala."

"Mr. Thorpe," the commissioner wavered, "Mr. Thorpe, will you—do you—"

They waited for what Ben Thorpe would say. In all that press of men, there probably was not one who didn't understand what was happening here, who could not see the long miles of deep grass of the Crying Wolf, the bawling herds, the turn of a struggle that was as long and as old as the Chisholm trail.

Ben Thorpe's face was expressionless as he got up from his chair, but men pushed back, stumbled over each other to get out of his way, as he walked down the length of that packed room and out into the street.

The deputy commissioner seemed to have melted down, unrecognizable now as the crisp little man who had opened the bidding. His face was white and set, and his eyes showed fear.

"Well?" said King.

"The Crying Wolf," the commissioner said huskily, "the Crying Wolf lands—if—if there are no other bids—go to King-Gordon . . ."

Something like a sigh, a general release of tension, ran through that jam of men.

Close to Dusty King's ear, Bill Roper asked out of the side of his mouth, "How high would we—how high could we have gone?"

The mask of Dusty King's face broke up as every muscle in his face came into action, and every tooth showed as he grinned. Through those good teeth, he spat tobacco juice on the floor.

"Seventy cents," King answered him.

CHAPTER THREE

An hour spent in the Wells Fargo office with the deputy commissioner, filling out forms, signing papers, ended as Dusty King and Bill Roper stood with Lew Gordon on the boardwalk in the late afternoon sunlight. It was the first time the three had had a word alone since the Crying Wolf had passed into the hands of King-Gordon.

"Well," said Dusty King, "we got her."

"We paid high, Dusty," Gordon said.

"But we got her!"

"And we can use her." For once, Lew Gordon's eyes, grave and thoughtful still, seemed to be looking past the immediate; he seemed to be seeing beyond the muddy, thronged street of the little town, beyond the loading corrals where the cattle bawled, beyond the long reaches of the prairie. He was not a man who saw visions, but perhaps he was seeing part of one now.

"Maybe," he said, "this is our chance. Maybe now we can get the cow business on a sound basis, here in the north, and have some order, and decent law."

"You'll never get a 'sound basis' until Ben Thorpe is bust'," Dusty said. "What law enforcement we got in the West is rotten through and through with office holders that Thorpe owns.

Look at this deputy commissioner, here. He'd have broke every law in the calendar to give Ben Thorpe that land."

"Someday," Gordon said slowly, "Ben Thorpe has got to go."

"Someday, hell! Lew, we've got him beat!"

Lew Gordon, the slow-moving seeker of peace, did not have Dusty's talent for celebration. "God knows I hope so, Dusty."

King's exuberant mood of victory was not to be dampened. He was walking on air, so that the deep heels of his hoots hardly touched the boards. "You want law and order?" he chortled. "We'll show 'em law and order!"

"That puts me in mind," said Gordon. "A feller passed me this here to give to you." He handed Dusty King a little twisted scrap of paper, torn off the corner of something else. Dusty untangled it, looked at it a moment, and showed it to the others. Five words were penciled on it in sprawling black letters:

IN GOD'S NAME LOOK OUT

"Who's this from, Lew?"

Gordon's lips moved almost soundlessly. "Dry Camp Pierce."

Roper knew that name, without knowing what lengths of outlawry had brought Dry Camp Pierce to where he was today. Rewards backed by Ben Thorpe were on Dry Camp's scalp over half the West. It was probably as much as his life was worth to show himself in Ogallala now.

"This note—"

Dusty King tossed it off with a shrug. "Oh—I suppose Thorpe is getting drunk somewhere and spouting off about what all he's going to do to me, when he catches up." Dusty's teeth showed in his infectious grin. "I suppose Dry Camp thought I ought to know about it."

"He's right, Dusty," Lew Gordon said. "We do want to look out, all of us, all the time."

"We always had to look out," Dusty scoffed.

"It'll be the more so now. There isn't anything in the world Ben Thorpe's people will stop at, Dusty."

"Let 'em come on."

"We want to look out," Gordon said again.

"If you feel that way about it," said Dusty, "what was the idea of your working through that law we can't wear guns in town?"

Bill Roper said, "We could have brought it to an open shoot-out, five years ago—ten years ago. Better if we had."

Gordon shook his head. "Nothing ever gets fixed up with guns."

Dusty King pulled his hat a little more on one side so that he could wink at Bill Roper unobserved. But he said, "He's partly right, Bill. Ben Thorpe isn't just one man anymore. Walk

Lasham—Cleve Tanner—any one of a dozen others could step into his shoes. It's the whole rotten organization that has to be busted up."

"Ben Thorpe downed, and they'll quit," Bill Roper said.

"Ben Thorpe down and it's only begun," Dusty countered. "Get it out of your head that you can fix anything up by downing Ben Thorpe. Not while his organization stands in one piece, reaching all over hell's creation. Might be a good idea for you to remember that, Bill, in case anything happens."

"Dusty," Bill said, "if ever they get you, by God, I'll get Ben Thorpe if it's the last—"

"No," said Dusty. "You hear me? No. If they get me—you'll remember what I said. You remember you're fighting a thing, and a big one, not just one man." His face crinkled in that familiar, contagious grin. "Forget it! Dry Camp's spooky, that's all. Bill, you go on up to the house and tell Jody that there's going to be some new cow faces in the Crying Wolf—under King-Gordon brands. Me and Lew's going to take a walk through the town."

He hooked an arm through his partner's and went swaggering off.

Ten paces down the walk, he stopped, turned, and came back. He leaned close to Roper. "If anything should happen, kid—remember what I said."

CHAPTER FOUR

That Lew Gordon had a daughter was not so surprising as that he had only one. Coming from a race of two-bottle, four-wife men, Lew Gordon had turned out a little different from the rest. Single-minded, like an old eagle or a wolf, he clung all his life to the memory of the wife he had lost when their first child was born.

Jody Gordon was twenty now. She didn't exactly run Lew Gordon; nobody did that. But it was fairly apparent that his stubborn bid for supremacy in western cattle was intended on her behalf, and without her, would have been meaningless to him.

Since King-Gordon had been making a definite stand in the north, Lew had built Jody a house in Ogallala that was just about the showplace of the northern plains. In a city, it would not have looked like much, but here in the muddy cow town, where everything had to come from a long way, it was a triumph and an imposing sight. Lew Gordon had designed it himself—a big two-story frame structure, painted white, and decorated with miles of scroll-sawed gingerbread. And it supported no less than four of the curious wooden towers that residential architecture sprouted during the Ulysses S. Grant period.

The whole thing was enclosed by a little white picket fence, as if this man of vast spaces and uncounted herds had felt it necessary to mark off for Jody Gordon, in the middle of all that raw land, a little space where civilization should be.

Because Gordon hadn't wanted his girl filtering around through the press of Ben Thorpe's ruffians at the auction, getting his own boys into fights, Jody Gordon was waiting here for news of what had happened to the Crying Wolf. Bill Roper vaulted the foolish little picket gate, scuffed the mud off his boots on the high front steps, and let himself in. He sent a Comanche war gobble ringing through the house, but Jody was already flying into the room.

"Did you get it? Did you get it?"

"Sure, we got it."

"Much of it?"

"All of it!"

Jody flung herself at him and kissed him, so sweet, so vital, so completely feminine that he wanted to keep her close to him. But she broke away again as he tried to hold her.

"How much did it cost?"

"Seventy cents—gold."

Jody's breath caught. "Can we come out on it?"

"Sure, we can come out on it. Not a cent less would've turned the trick. Dusty—"

Bill Roper hardly ever expressed his deep-rooted admiration for everything Dusty King did, but now it brought the story tumbling out of him. The edgy, short-worded interchanges at the scene of the auction came now to Jody as what they were—passages in an all-important struggle, with the nonchalant King out-thinking, out-tricking, out-powering his enemy—tying him in knots.

Jody sat on a walnut table that had come all the way from St. Louis and swung her feet. The story seemed to tickle her in more ways than one. "I can just see you all," she said, "standing around making an impression on each other."

She had gotten away from Bill Roper in the past few years, not because they wished it that way but because he had been on the trails with Dusty, or else Jody—more rarely Bill himself—had been away somewhere for a little schooling. Though no year ever passed without his seeing her two or three times, their total time together, added up, could not have amounted to more than a couple of weeks. Lately, it seemed to him that she had gathered up all the laughter that her father had lost along the way. An irrepressible twinkle was always working into her eyes, and she turned everything into nonsense.

"Dusty seems to have done right well," Jody drawled. "And what were you doing all this time?"

"Me? Why—I was just standing there."

"With your mouth open?"

"Why on earth would my mouth be open?"

"Oh, I don't know, but I was hoping—you see, you look so kind of sweet, standing around with your mouth open."

"Well—it was about all I could do. This was Dusty's game, from start to finish."

"Start to finish, eh?"

"Why, sure. He—"

"And all you did was ride about fifty million miles in three weeks, and cover the Crying Wolf backwards and forward and across to make an estimate on—"

"Well, that didn't accomplish anything."

"Not anything at all?"

"Shucks, no. We—"

"There's a picture!" Jody said. "Billy Roper flogging horses in circles by the week—not accomplishing a thing. I might have known it."

"Well—of course, I did kind of take a look at the grass."

"That was smart," said Jody respectfully. "That was real smart. Did you try eating some of it?"

"Nope. I did pick some and saved it, figuring to make a hen's nest later, but I lost hold of it swimming Elk River. What the heck's the matter with you, anyway?"

Roper turned his back on her, tired of her unconcealed mockery. As he stood staring out the window, the curtains made him feel as if he had cobwebs in his eyes, and he started to strike them aside but did not. For all he knew, they would come down on him, or tear. Southward as far as he could see, the prairie was stripped bare by the close cropping of held herds—a soggy brown waste. But beyond, where the grass began, beyond vision from here, the broad, deep-cut tracks ran south—the many-branched, vague wanderings of the Great Trail . . .

Two, three more days now, and he and Dusty would be heading south on that trail, Dusty to meet Windy Thompson, now pressing north, somewhere on that long trail with four thousand head from Texas, Bill himself to meet Jack Harper, still farther back, with twenty-five hundred more. Months out with the cattle—

He turned from the window, and she was laughing at him as he had thought, her mouth smothered with her fingers.

"Come here a minute," he said, going toward her.

"What for?"

She twisted from the edge of the table, as if to put it between them, but she was too late. His rope-hard fingers caught her wrist and held her as easily as if he had dallied a calf to the horn.

"Listen—" he begged her. "Listen—"

He caught her up, clamped an arm behind her head, and kissed her hard. Hard, and for a long time.

So long as she was rigid in his arms, fighting him, he held her, but when she stood limp, neither yielding nor resisting, his arms relaxed, and Jody tore herself free. She lashed out at him like a little mustang, striking him across the mouth. Her face was white, all that quick, irrepressible laughter gone, as for a moment she looked at him. A trickle of blood ran from Bill Roper's lips and made a crooked mark on his chin. Then she turned and fled.

When she was gone, Bill Roper stood still, sucking his cut lips. After a little while, he went to the window, instinctively turning to open space for his answers, as his breed inevitably did, always.

He could remember Jody Gordon as a little tow-headed kid, before her hair had darkened into the elusive misty brown that it was now. Or as a colt-legged girl with scratches on her shins from riding bare-legged through the sage. Or as a peculiarly tempestuous, uncertain thing, neither child nor woman. But this latest phase he couldn't understand at all.

He picked up his hat and, for a little while, stood turning it in his hands. Then he threw it in the corner and went searching through the house.

Jody was in the tallest of the four foolish towers. From here, you could see the town and the slim, glittering line of the railroad, connecting these far plainsmen with a world hungry for beef. The town sprawled neither compactly nor with self-confidence, but it drew in tightly to the loading chutes, as if it knew that the rails were its life. Beyond, you saw the prairie. Already the many threads of the Long Trail were bitten into it so deep that no hoeman would ever again completely stir up that hoof-hammered ground . . .

Jody said matter-of-factly, "We've got to have more loading pens, Bill."

Bill's face broke into a slow grin. Abruptly, he laid hard hands on disused sashes and broke them open. Into their little cubicle flowed the sweet air of the open prairie sweep, inspiriting with the fresh smell of the new grass.

She said, "Tell me about your new job."

"It isn't new."

"They said that you'd be the new boss of the Crying Wolf, if we got it."

For more years than he could remember, he had been working toward this opportunity—the chance to take two years, or three, with such-and-such cattle, on such-and-such land, and show that he could pay out on market deliveries in pounds of beef. But now—a million horns and hoofs didn't seem to mean so much.

Something was here—something that wasn't anyplace else—not on the long trail, not in the wild terminal towns. He knew now he had to tell her that, and he dreaded it, because she probably would think it was funny. He wouldn't look at her as he spoke, because he didn't want to see her laughing at him.

"I don't know as I'm so much interested as I was," he said.

"Why, Billy—not interested in the Crying Wolf—nearly five hundred square miles of feeder land! What's come over you?"

"I guess maybe I'm tired of riding alone," Bill said.

"Alone? With all the outfit you'll have—I wouldn't call it alone."

"I would."

He still didn't look at her, and she couldn't see what was in his eyes. All she could see was his profile; a profile at once young and somehow craggy—strong, easy, watchful, accustomed to a lot of grinning. This youngster was the Long Trail itself. Banjos were the music in his brain, and the thud of hoofs and the bawling of cattle made up the rhythms of his life. The profile Jody looked at now had been lighted by a thousand far, lost campfires before he was twenty.

"Grass country is lonely country," he said now, "as lonely as the dry plains. You get to wondering what the everlasting cattle add up to in the course of a life. Then some night you know you don't care what they add up to, and you think, '*Damn fat beef!*' "

"Why, Billy—why, Billy—"

"None of it means a damn, without you're there," he told her. "Working cattle doesn't mean anything, because you'll always have all the cattle you need anyway. And no long trail means anything without you at the end of it. I'm sick of long drive-trails, empty of you at the end."

There was a long, motionless silence. He kept his eyes on the far sand hills as presently she leaned forward to look up into his face.

"You really mean it, don't you?" Jody said.

Down in the town, a fusillade of pistol shots rattled, and they could hear the whoops of cowboys celebrating the fact that they were alive.

Jody's words came very faintly and a little breathless.

"Why didn't you say so before?"

He looked at her then, and she wasn't laughing. In her eyes was a new, grave light, such as he had never seen; a warm light, a beloved light, better than sunset to a weary day-rider who has worked leather since before dawn. Timorously, but very willingly, she came into his arms, and he held her as if she were not only a very precious but a very fragile thing. For a little while, it seemed that one trail, a trail longer than the Long Trail itself, had come to its end.

"Can't believe," he said at last, his lips in her hair, "you're sure enough mine."

"All yours—all, all!"

"Forever?"

"Oh, my darling! Longer than you'll ever be mine . . ."

They had one hour, there in the prairie lookout

tower, discovering each other, getting acquainted as if for the first time. The sun went down in a tremendous welter of color—a medicine sunset, such as made the Sioux read spirit signs. A cool, gently fading light painted the sandhills red-gold on one side, and smoky lavender on the other, and through the dusk, lights winked up at them from the town. Another short fusillade of gunfire spoke, somewhere down there among the wooden buildings.

Jody shivered a little. "I wish Dad and Dusty would come. Especially Dusty."

"Why?"

"He has so many enemies. Some of them are dangerous as diamond-backs. It worries me when he's due and doesn't get back."

"Dusty'll take care of himself."

"I thought the town ordinance barred out gun-toting."

"It does. But some of the boys brush over that. Don't you fret, honey. Dusty's all right."

"Just the same, I wish he'd come."

Bill Roper chuckled and held her closer. "I hope he never comes!" She settled deeper into his arms.

One half hour more . . .

Up from the town came a crazily ridden horse, splashing mud eaves-high under the urge of spur and quirt.

"He'll lame his pony if he goes down in that

slick," Bill commented. "Now what do you suppose—"

The rider tried to pull up in front of the house, and the frantic pony swerved and slid, mouth wide open to the sky. Its shoulder crashed the fence, taking down a dozen feet of pickets. The rider tumbled off, ran up the steps to hammer on the door.

"Bill! Bill Roper!"

"Let him holler," Bill said.

"No—find out what he wants. Maybe it's—"

"Oh, all right."

Roper went clattering down the stairs, pulled open the door. "Now listen, you—"

"Bill—Dusty—Mr. King—he—"

Bill Roper froze, and there was a long moment of paralyzed silence. "Spit it out, man!" Roper shouted at him.

"Bill—he's daid!"

"Who—who—"

"Dusty King's daid! Bill, they gunned him—they gunned him down!"

"Who did?"

"Tain't known. Mr. Gordon's there. He—"

"Dusty King—you sure it's him that's dead?"

"Daid sartin. Nobody knows how, or who, yet."

Bill Roper walked out past the cowboy stiffly, like a man gone blind. Without knowing what he did he walked down to the gate and stood gripping the pickets with his two hands. He was hearing his own words, "I hope he never—"

He wanted a smoke, he wanted a chew, but he just stood there like a wooden man.

This spring the northern grass would come rich and deep, and the backs of ten thousand cattle would be steaming as they fattened in the spring warmth . . . but in all that sunlight—Dusty swaggering—never more—

CHAPTER FIVE

They buried Dusty King five miles south of Ogallala, beside the Great Trail which he himself had pioneered. They thought he would want to rest out there in the open plain, near enough to the cattle trail so that the rumble of hoofs would sometimes come to him through the ground.

Over his grave they piled boulders, after the fashion of the prairie men. Bill Roper himself fitted a cross of railroad ties, the most durable and massive timber available at Ogallala.

After that was all done, and night had come on, and everybody had gone back to town, Bill Roper went back to that lonely cross and squatted on his heels against the pile of stone. He was smoking cigarettes that he rolled and recalling things—kid memories—that he had not thought of for a long time. He remembered Dusty's long patience in teaching him the Indian sign language. He remembered Dusty setting his broken arm, when Bill, eight years old then, had somersaulted his horse in the Black Butte rocks.

After a while, he was even able to remember the first time he had seen Dusty King. The thundering slam of hoofs, the crashing of long rifles, the shouting, the terror of disaster, his own father's voice—all that was a blur. Then the long stillness while the little boy lay hidden, waiting for the call that could never come. At last, other different men and horses . . .

Perhaps nobody in the world but Dusty King could have sensed that little presence. But presently, a big bristle-faced man in a slouch hat and worn saddle clothes dropped on his knees and held out his arms to the blank brush . . . and the little boy ran out to cling sobbing to the rawhide trail driver, Dusty King.

Roper sat there a long time, and the butts of his brown-paper cigarettes made a little litter at the foot of Dusty's pile of stone.

After a while, a ridden horse came toward the cross at a walk, and Bill Roper put out his smoke and remained motionless, unseen against the stones, as the horseman came up.

The rider stepped to the ground and walked slowly toward the cross, the reins of his pony on his arm.

"Well?" Roper said at last.

The effect of that single word was explosive. In the next split second, the horseman had vaulted into the saddle, and the thin starlight showed on the barrel of his sky-raised gun.

"*Quién es*?"

Roper said, "Oh, hello, Dry Camp."

The rider's gun slapped back into its holster. Swinging down again, the wiry little man known as Dry Camp Pierce came and sat down beside Bill at the foot of the stones.

"Find out anything in the town?"

"Hell, no."

"No," Dry Camp repeated after him. "No, and they won't."

"You talk mighty sure, Dry Camp."

"I talk mighty sure because I am mighty sure. Nobody saw Dusty killed except the three men that done it, and one other man."

Bill Roper's hand shot out and caught Dry Camp's lean arm in a grip that bit like a trap. "Who was that?"

"Me."

There was a silence, sharp and hard, before Bill said, "You were there, and you didn't—"

"What could I do? I had no gun."

Bill Roper let his hand drop away. Out on the plain a coyote yammered, serenading the night.

"Way I'm fixed," Dry Camp grunted, "I got to keep my horns pulled in. They got a law there against gun-toting in town. They don't all mind it, but I got to mind it. I've been checking my gunbelt every time I go into the damned town."

"How in hell is it you haven't told anybody this?"

"Haven't had any chance to talk to you," Dry Camp said. "I'm telling you now, ain't I? Who the hell else would I tell?"

"Lew Gordon—"

"Lew Gordon be damned! It was him got that law against gun-toting put through. If it wasn't for that I'd have got a couple of the bastards. Or tried."

"Who was it?"

"Cleve Tanner, and Walk Lasham, and Ben Thorpe."

Dry Camp took a match out of the pocket cow his cowhide vest and chewed the end.

"You see—" he searched for his words painfully, after the manner of men who are much alone—"Dusty, he tied his horse out back of the Lone Star Bar, in the angle of the wagon shed. There's a kind of a corner there, like you can't see into it from any place, hardly, and what with it getting dark—"

"Where were you?"

"I was in Bailey's Harness Shop, next door. I saw Dusty turn off the boardwalk and walk back between the buildings. I'd been watching for him, because I wanted to speak to him a minute. I went back through the harness shop, and I was just going out the back door. And then hell bust in the wagon shed angle."

"The time it happened," Bill Roper said, "there must have still been a little light."

"Enough to see by, all right. These three varmints steps out of the shed quick and quiet. Dusty knew what he was up against, all right. His gun come out, but Walk Lasham grabs his gun arm with his left hand and bears down like he was wrastling him. Then the whole works seems to blow up as all three of 'em let loose. They just stood and throwed it into him, and it seemed like he was never going to fall. Ben Thorpe pumped two more shots after Dusty was down, and dead."

That was all the story. Both of them seemed to recognize that there were no questions to ask, nothing to add.

"I promise you this, Bill," Dry Camp said at last. "I can't go up and testify against these men. You know why. If I let it be known that I'm here, that's the finish of me. But that would be all right. Only, what court, that we got, would believe me against them?"

Bill Roper said, "There isn't anything you can do, I don't suppose."

"Oh, yes, there is. There's one thing I can do. I'll have to kind of bide my time, and make it sure, but—I'm going to get me these three men."

"No, you ain't," Bill Roper said. "We're going to go at this thing a different way."

"What different way is there to go? I know how you feel, Bill—like as if you wanted 'em yourself. But you're young, and you got a future, and you got a girl. It's different with me. You and Lew Gordon go on your way—I'll go mine."

"Trouble with you," Bill Roper said, "you're figuring these three men as just three men. They ain't. They got the biggest string of tough outfits in the country, and they spread all the way from the Rio Grande to the Rosebud, and beyond. We got to bust up the whole works, if we want to get any place."

Dry Camp shrugged. "That's no job for a couple of outlaw punchers, Bill. And it ain't work for you and Lew Gordon, neither. You got to fight fire with fire. Lew Gordon won't do that. King-Gordon could be twice as strong as Thorpe, and Thorpe would hold the whole works off with one hand."

"It's different now."

"How is it different?"

"I'm the King half of King-Gordon," Roper said.

Dry Camp was silent for several minutes. "What you aim to do?"

"I aim to start in Texas, where Cleve Tanner runs Thorpe's breeding outfits in the Big Bend. I aim to tie into him piece by piece, till Ben Thorpe is smashed out of the West."

"Lew Gordon will never stand for—"

"Then, by God, King-Gordon has come to its split-up!"

Silence again before Dry Camp said, "And I suppose I'm expected to just kind of stand aside and stay out of it and see how you work it out, huh? Well, I won't do it, Bill."

"You're in this, Dry Camp."

"How am I in it?"

"I've got to have me an outfit. It's got to be made up of boys that aren't afraid of Ben Thorpe or all hell, boys that haven't got anything more to lose. I'll need near fifty men. But to start off with, I want Lee Harnish, and Tex Daniels, and Tex Long, Nate Liggett—Dave Shannon—"

"Wow!" said Dry Camp.

"What's the matter?"

"You get those four or five in the same bunch, they'll eat each other alive."

"That's the kind I want," Bill Roper said. "I want a wild bunch such as the West has never seen before."

"And me—what am I supposed to do?"

"You—you're heading south. You're going back to Texas and you're going to start rounding 'em in."

"What you offering these boys?"

"Horses and grub, and what other stuff we'll need. Not another damned thing. I'll see you again before you go. We'll know by then whether King-Gordon is making this fight, or if I split off on my own."

"You sure you want to do this, Bill?"

"I know what I want to do."

They sat silent for a long time more.

"All right," Dry Camp said. "I'll go."

CHAPTER SIX

In the starlight, Bill Roper swung down in front of the little shack which served King-Gordon as a loading-foreman's office at their Ogallala pens. This was the little saddle-cluttered room in which Dusty King and Lew Gordon had come to the decision which brought King-Gordon the Crying Wolf lands—and cost Dusty King his life. Within, four or five lanterns were lit, and here Bill Roper found Lew Gordon sitting alone.

"The sheriff and the United States Marshal just left," Gordon said. "You ought to have tried to be here, Bill."

"Anything get done?"

"Well, no, nobody knows anything, beyond what we all guess."

"I just talked to a man," Roper said, "that saw the killing."

Gordon was instantly alert. "Who was it?"

"He's a man that can't come forward, because he's already an outlaw in his own right. But Dusty was killed by Ben Thorpe, and Walk Lasham, and Cleve Tanner, the three working together. Walk Lasham bore down Dusty's gun."

They looked at each other for a long moment.

"I figured they hired it done," Gordon said.

"Seems not."

"This man that told you this—we've got to get

hold of him. His story has to go to the authorities, Bill."

Roper shook his head. "He'll hang if they lay hands on him. Anyway, nobody would believe him against these three."

Lew Gordon made a gesture at once impatient and weary. "Wherever we turn we hit some snag of lawlessness," he said. "There's too many men afraid to stand forward and face out the law. Seems like nothing is done open and aboveboard anymore."

"Never was, since I remember," Roper said.

"I suppose," Gordon said at last, "this is just another case where there isn't anything we can do. But I swear to heaven, Bill, I'll get Ben Thorpe in the end! Somehow I'll find ways to drag him down, someday, if it takes my last cent."

"I've got a couple of ways in mind right now," Roper said. "I'm going on the warpath, Lew."

Gordon had been fiddling with a pencil, and now he threw it on the table in front of him. "We're figuring you to take over the Crying Wolf, Bill. Dusty's half of King-Gordon naturally will stand in your name now; Dusty never paid any attention to any other kin. But the Crying Wolf was where he figured for you to go and work, and there isn't any call to change that, now."

"You can count me out of the Crying Wolf, Lew."

"What do you want to do?"

"We're going to branch out a new way," Roper said. "We're going to have a warrior outfit. And I'm its new boss."

"I don't get you."

"We're going to carry the war into the other camp, Lew. For every outfit that Ben Thorpe has grabbed by force of arms, he's going to lose two. For every head that has come into his herds by rustle and raid, two head of his are going to be missing when he makes his roundup count. First thing, I'm going to break Cleve Tanner down in Texas. After that—"

Lew Gordon looked Bill Roper hard in the eye, smiled a little, and shook his head. His voice was slow and deep, stubbornly emphatic, as a granite cliff is emphatic. "No. We've never gone outside the law yet, and while I live we never will. We play the straight game always, and if we lose—that's in the hands of things beyond us."

Bill Roper angered. "I know how you feel about it," he said, keeping his voice down. "You swayed Dusty that way always. If you'd looked at it different, the guns would have been out years ago—and it would have been Ben Thorpe that went down. As it is—Dusty King is dead. Now you want me to drift on as we always drifted on, and I'm supposed to forget that Dusty's out there under a pile of stones. Well, I'm not going to play it that way, Gordon."

“While you’re with King-Gordon,” Lew said slowly, “you’ll play it as I say you’ll play it.”

Their eyes met and held, and Roper knew that he still respected this man. Quiet, peaceful, seeking always the un-warlike way, Lew Gordon was sometimes misunderstood. But Bill Roper knew now, as he had always known, that there was no fear in this man, and no weakness, but only a tremendous, unshakable loyalty to a set of principles for which the plains were perhaps not ready.

“If you want to buy me out,” Roper said, “you can do it at your own price. Because I’m going to do exactly what I tell you I’m going to do. I wouldn’t run a sneak on you, Lew.”

“You figure,” Lew Gordon said incredulously, “that you, one youngster on horseback, can smash up Ben Thorpe? You wouldn’t last forty seconds longer than a celluloid collar on a dead gambler.”

“There’ll be a few go with me,” Roper said.

“Who?”

“Dry Camp Pierce, for one. Lee Harnish, Tex Daniels, Tex Long . . . in all, maybe fifty men that I think I know where to get.”

Lew Gordon looked as if he would explode. “You’re naming the most vicious outlaws on the plains,” he said. “If you ever get those men together, it will be the most infernal wild bunch that ever—”

"By God," said Bill Roper, "I'll show you how to clean a range or break a range. I'm telling you I don't care which."

Lew Gordon slapped his hand on the table; it fell with a dull and heavy wallop, but so hard it seemed the top of the table would split.

"No! No, by God! Not under my brand. Not in a hundred years . . ."

"Then draw up the terms of the sale."

Lew Gordon studied him, then. "You're all lathered up, Bill," he said. "You're lathered and upset—"

"Am I?"

Gordon made a gesture of futility, for Bill Roper looked as hard and cool as anything he had ever seen. "If you want to split off, I can't stop you," he said at last. "But you're leaving behind you a great opportunity, and the beginning of a future any man might envy. You could be a cattle power, someday, in your own right, or governor of a state, or—anything you wanted to be. You're throwing over all that, and—other things. Bill, are you thinking of that?"

"I'm thinking of a man," said Bill. "A man that's dead."

Gordon was silent again for a long time. He seemed very old, very tired. "Reckon you're man enough to make your own decisions, Bill."

"Thanks, Lew."

"But do me one last favor—will you? Don't

decide here and now. Take a couple of days to think it over. It's for your own good. But I'm asking it as a favor to me . . ."

Bill Roper dropped his eyes, and for a moment or two he hesitated.

"I'll take an hour," he decided in compromise.

CHAPTER SEVEN

Bill Roper walked slowly to the Gordons' tall house, on its rise at the edge of the town, and let himself in softly. He wanted desperately to talk to Jody Gordon, but it was nearly midnight, and he couldn't make up his mind to wake her.

As it happened, decision was unnecessary. In the fireplace some lengths of cottonwood log still burned, and before the fire Jody lounged upon a buffalo robe, wide awake. She was stretched full length, her hands clasped behind her head, but as he came into the room, she extended both arms to him and smiled.

"You've been a long time."

"I know." He stopped beside her, half raised her in his arms, and kissed her lingeringly. Her arms and her lips clung, making it difficult for him to think of the road he had chosen. But presently he sat beside her on the buffalo robe and turned his eyes to the coals.

"There's some stuff we have to talk about, Jody."

"I can think of better things to do with firelight than just talk."

"Jody—King-Gordon is splitting up."

Jody brought herself up on one elbow. "Why, Bill—what do you mean?"

"Dusty's share comes to me, as you know. I—I'm taking it out."

"You're—Bill, you must be loco!"

"Maybe. I'm going against Ben Thorpe."

"But—but—" Jody was at a loss for words.

"Since the trail began, he's stood for everything we re against. Four of the biggest rustling gangs in the country are directly hooked up with him, if it could be proved. He's stopped at nothing, and where he couldn't force his way he's bought his way. But now—he's gone too far."

He glanced at her, and her startled face was very lovely, highlighted by the little fire. He laced his hands together to stop their shaking. "Tonight I told your father what I'm going to do. My idea is to give Thorpe his own medicine and force it down him until he's finished—a wild bunch of our own, tougher than his, made up of men that hate him to the ground."

"And then—?"

"Raid and counter-raid, and what he's taken, take back! Until his credit busts, and his varmints drop from around him, and he's just one man, so that another man can walk against him with a six-gun, and know that when that's done he's finished for sure . . ."

"Bill, are you crazy? You can't—you can't—"

His voice was bleak; it could hardly be heard. He was looking at his hands. "We've talked too many years of what couldn't be done, or how. Until now, Dusty's out there tonight, under that stone pile—and still nothing to be done. I reckon it's my turn to ride, now."

"You'd quit King-Gordon—quit Dad—to go on a crazy wild-bunch raid—"

"There'll be more raids than one. A hundred raids, if I live. Jody, I swear to you, I'll never quit until this thing is done."

"But—all his outfits—his sheriffs, his men—"

"They'll quit, as he breaks. I'm going after Cleve Tanner first, in the Big Bend, and when I'm through with him, Thorpe won't be able to throw a feeder herd on the trail. Then Walk Lasham, in the north, where they're already hurt for lack of the Crying Wolf—until—"

His words were monotoned, but Jody Gordon, bred and born to the gaunt Texan plains, knew what a wild bunch was, and what it meant to go against Ben Thorpe by his own means. Perhaps in the flicker of the firelight she could see the silent night-riders moving in the starlight, their rifles in their hands. And perhaps, for a moment, the distant bawling of cattle, which came to them even here, became the voicing of hard-pressed herds, moved on the dead run between dusk and sunrise.

Jody said, "And—what about us?"

"Us?"

"You and me?"

"Jody, I was hoping—I was hoping you'd swing with me."

"What way is there for me to swing with you?"

"This may take a long time, but it won't take forever. Someday all these war clouds will be cleared away. And—if you could see it my way, maybe you'd let me come back to you then."

There seemed to be no breath in Jody's voice. "I'm supposed to wait around, and think well of you, while you gang with the wild bunch in a crazy, useless feud that you can't win?"

In the uncertain light of the fire, Bill Roper's eyes could not be seen, his face a mask painted by the embers. He found nothing that he could say.

Suddenly, Jody flared up. Her eyes blazed, and her hair streamed back from her face as she sat up, as if she rode in the wind.

"You can't, you can't! I won't let you—it isn't fair, nor right, nor decent—"

"It's what I have to do."

Jody stopped as if she had been struck. When she spoke again her voice was low and even, and so stony hard that he would not have recognized it.

"I don't believe you. I think tomorrow you'll be telling me that all this isn't so. But if you do mean it—if you go on and do as you say—then you and I are through, and I don't want to see you again, or hear your voice. We—we had everything . . . and you're throwing it all away . . ."

The firelight caught the glint of her tears, and she turned away, head up, with a toss of her hair so that its brown mist hid her face from him.

Bill didn't say anything. He had turned gray-faced, and he stared into the coals. Presently, as he watched the fire, he saw again a rift of brush in which a little boy hid like a rabbit, and a gently grinning face that was through with grinning now. He thought of Dry Camp's story, "Seemed like he'd never fall . . ."

Roper got up silently and went out of the house.

CHAPTER EIGHT

Lew Gordon was playing solitaire when Bill Roper got back to the little shack by the loading pens. Roper took off his hat, tossed it aside, and sat down.

"We can just as well figure up the terms of the split."

"What did Jody say?"

"She's quitting me, Lew."

"What the devil else can you expect her to do, if you go on with this wild, stubborn—"

"I couldn't expect anything else."

Lew Gordon looked baffled. Obviously, he had counted on Jody to turn back Bill Roper.

"You ready to draw up the terms?"

"Hardly seems it can be done in a minute. It'll take a few days to—"

"I'm leaving in the morning. My terms are few and simple. You can work out the details any way that suits yourself."

Once more, as if needing time, Lew Gordon got out the worn tally book and put his glasses on. For a moment or two he thumbed through the dog-eared pages. Then abruptly he flung the tally book away and spread his hands on the table before him.

"Let's hear your idea of it."

"I don't figure to take much with me," Roper said. "But there are some things I need. First thing, I want seven of our camps in Texas."

Lew Gordon stared at the table, picked up a pencil, fidgeted with it. "Which ones?"

"I want the Pot Hook camp, and the winter camp of the Three Bar, and the southwest outpost of the old Bar-Circle. I want two of the border camps. Willow Creek will do for one, and the Dry Saddle Crossing will do for the other. I want the new Bull Wagon camp, and the K-G horse ranch at Stillwater."

"The brands are going to be terrible mixed up," Gordon said.

"I'm only taking such cattle as are running under odd brands. All our regular brands stay with you. I've placed my camps so that your stock can be worked as before. Except maybe the Pot Hook, and we'll come to some special deal—"

Gordon threw his pencil down. "You're not getting anything out of this that anybody can use," he declared.

"I think I'll know how to use it. Later on, I'll send you a list of the northern camps I want. They'll amount to about the same as the ones I want in Texas."

"It sure sounds to me like you're wanting me to buy you out in cash," Gordon said. "And if that's what's in your mind—I can't do it, Bill. There just ain't the money."

"There won't be any trouble about that. In Texas, I may need up to fifty thousand dollars, but I don't have to have it now, and I don't have to have it all at once. It'll work out easy enough, Lew."

Even the rough provisional terms that they were noting here provided innumerable complications. In the next few hours, as they worked it out, many a consideration came up that Bill Roper hadn't thought of. It was near morning before Roper left to seek out Dry Camp Pierce.

CHAPTER NINE

Bill Roper headed south shortly after sunrise. He rode a tough buckskin pony and led a raw-boned black pack mule. In his pack and saddle bags were all the equipment and supplies he would need until he got to Bishop's Store, deep on his way. At his thigh was his forty-four six-gun, tied down with rawhide whang. In his saddle boot was the carbine he had used since he was fourteen years old.

Today, Dry Camp would be going east by railroad, beginning the long roundabout way which would bring him to Texas long before Bill. With Dry Camp Pierce went letters to the foremen at Willow Creek and the Pot Hook, who knew him already. With these camps as a secure base, Pierce was to begin the missionary work which would lay the foundations for Bill Roper's wild bunch. On the same train with Dry Camp, but not with him, would go certain dispatches which would give Bill Roper temporary credit with Wells Fargo in the south, until the affairs of King-Gordon could be ultimately settled.

Roper himself took the direct but slow trail because on his way he wished to pick up word of certain men whom perhaps only he could find.

Lew Gordon had shaken hands with him

gravely at his departure; an uncomfortable job for Bill, which he was glad to get over with. For all he knew, he would never meet Dusty King's old partner on friendly terms again. Half a dozen of the King-Gordon trail bosses and range foremen had got wind, and come down to the corrals, and he had had to go through the dismal ceremony of taking leave of them all, to the tune of witticisms that fell flat in the mud and there died.

More pestiferous, but shaken loose in the end, were a handful of malcontents from various King-Gordon outfits. In some mysterious way they had got the word that he was taking the war trail, and they rode with him a mile into the prairie, trying to persuade him that they ought to be counted in. He got rid of them all at last and was able to head south alone.

But Jody Gordon—he had not seen her again at all. He was thinking of her now as she had flared up at him the night before, warlike as a little eagle, but very lovely still, with the fire in her eyes . . . and the tune that he was whistling to his pony was a bitter tune, with cowboy words to it that did no credit to the song-maker's opinion of women.

Watchful always, as he had been taught to be almost before he could walk, his eye habitually caught the placement of distant dots that were grazing cattle or saddle stock; the far-off stir in the brush that was an Indian boy driving a cow;

a full mile away, a drifting speck that was a scavenging dog. Thus, he knew when, two miles off, a horseman dropped from a lookout just at the crest of a rise, and he knew that the rider had seen him and was moving to intercept his trail.

He thought, "I'll hear from this in between fifteen and twenty minutes."

No turn of events would have surprised him now that Dusty was dead. Since his intent was, evidently, already known, the sing of a bullet past his head was more to be expected than not. He shaped his track over open ground so that the unknown horseman should have the maximum difficulty in placing himself for a rifle shot from cover.

He did not have so long to wait as he had thought. No more than ten minutes had passed when the unknown rider came dusting around the shoulder of a sand hill and headed toward him at the dead run. Roper turned his horse broadside to the approach and waited. He slouched in his saddle, resting relaxed, but stiffened again as, at the furlong, he perceived the rider's identity.

The rider was Jody Gordon.

She appeared to have taken to the saddle in a hurry, for she wasn't wearing chaps, or anything else she should have been riding in, and her skirt was blowing back from her knees as she pulled up. What distance she had come, she had come fast, for her pony's flanks were heaving.

"You sure punish that horse," he said.

"I've got no call to save him. I'm not going anywhere."

There was a little silence, awkward for Bill Roper, as she sat and looked at him. The lower lids of her eyes were violet, so that he knew she had not slept, but he could not read her faintly smoky eyes. She was more pale than he had ever seen her, and the passivity of her face made her look like a little girl again.

"Sure sorry," he said, "that I didn't get to say goodbye to you. Didn't seem like you were any place around."

For a second or two the familiar twinkle seemed about to come into her eyes. "Did you hunt real hard?"

"Well—maybe I didn't. I guess it kind of seemed like we'd already said everything there was to be said."

"Maybe," she said slowly, "*I* didn't say everything I ought to have said."

He waited. After a moment or two, he snapped loose the black mule, restless on its lead, and it moved forward six lengths and went to grazing.

"I want you to know this," she said. "When you ride out of my life there isn't going to be anything left in it."

"Jody," he said, "are you trying to turn me back now?"

Her only answer was a little hopeless motion of her hands.

"Your father and I put in four hours last night, roughing out the terms of my split from King-Gordon. Think back yourself—did you ever see me turned back from something I figured I ought to do?"

She shook her head, and her face had even less color than before. "What did you say to my father?"

"What did he tell you I said?"

"That I—quit you."

"Well—didn't you?"

"Don't you know," she said crazily, "I wouldn't ever do that?"

He was silent, his eyes on his buckskin gloves as he adjusted his rope, the buckle of his rifle boot.

"I don't care anything about King-Gordon," Jody said. "I don't care whether you stay in King-Gordon, or get out, or where you go, or what you do. I'd go with you if you wanted me to go . . . And if you don't know that, you don't know anything at all!"

"Jody—you mean that?"

Jody Gordon swayed her shoulders as she sat there in the saddle; he had seen her father weave like that, many times, when he was up against something hard. Only, it seemed a very different thing as Jody did it.

"In King-Gordon, you were on the way to big things. But I don't care anything about that. Let the break-up with my father go through. Quit King-Gordon without two bits to your name. Take the least outpost camp there is under the brand and let him have the rest. I'll go with you, and stay with you, and I'll help you in every way I can to build something of our own."

Ahead on the prairie, the black mule cropped at the sparse cover. Working its way forward, slowly, it moved a full three lengths while Bill Roper still did not speak. He wanted to say something, anything, but he found he could not speak at all.

Jody said, almost hysterically, "Aren't you ever going to say anything?"

Bill Roper mumbled to his saddle horn, "Didn't know you felt that way . . . Wouldn't ever be any call—any reason—for you to let go all holts like that."

"Not any reason—?"

"King-Gordon—why, this outfit has a hold on the prairie all the way from—"

"I hate the prairie!" She was flaming up again, but not in the same way as the night before. Her voice was that of someone coming to the end of a string. "I hate these Godforsaken, barren wastes! I hate the fool cattle, and the trail-gaunted horses, and the bare, lonely ranches where nothing good ever comes!"

"Jody, someday we'll make this such a country as—"

"Oh, I know! I can see it just as you see it—just as you must see it. All the happy country, peaceful and quiet, some day, and no more long trails and no more wars—"

He started to say, "But first there's a couple of things—"

She was leaning toward him now, her voice gentle, coaxing, very tender. "Our own little old outfit—any outfit, and place—don't you see what a happy place we could make that be? A place where we could plant trees near the water, and watch them grow into big trees, and we'd be there together—"

To the south, the young sun crested the sand hills with long curving lines of gold, without seeming to bring any light. Through those sand hills threaded the long trail over which men pushed unhoping cattle, a long way and a hard way, full fifteen hundred miles. It was ill-defined, many miles wide, like the tracks of ships at sea—this dry, infinitely testing trail that Dusty King had been among the first to drive.

For men who had never been on that trail, it represented romance; for men who had been on it only once, it represented a memory of hell. Bill Roper knew it as it really was—hadn't he been raised on it? He knew the long monotony, the endless blocking of misfortune with wits and inadequate means, which was the true trail. Before him, that trail now stretched again. He would move faster than the cattle moved, but weeks would pass before he heard a human voice, months would roll out before he came to that long trail's end.

And after that—another trail, perhaps different, but perhaps so long that the long trail itself would be dwarfed to a stroll in the twilight, by comparison . . .

Roper shot a quick glance at Jody and immediately sent his eyes away again, as far as they could reach. Here was something he could not look at. It was as if everything men worked for, through drought, storm, night stampede, and fighting raid—everything for which men ever endured was here in one small form, not a horse length beyond the touch of his hands. If he had looked at her again, perhaps he would have kicked his pony stirrup to stirrup with hers and picked her out of the saddle, and kissed her mouth, and kept her close to him—then, and forever. But he sat motionless on his waiting pony.

"Look," he said at last—"Look—if you mean that, come with me. Come with me, now."

He could hardly hear her as she said, "Don't you think you ought to tell me where you're going?"

"Dry Camp Pierce is on his way, by a quicker

way than mine is. If he don't fall down, there'll be the start of a wild bunch waiting for me when I land in the Big Bend Country. I figure to take that bunch, build it, and add on. After that—well, you know what comes after that."

"And now, you're asking me to swing with that?"

"Jody, I've already told you what I've got to do."

The silence stretched out until you could have hung a saddle on it, and this time Bill's eyes were on Jody, and hers were on the saddle horn.

Slowly, she shook her head.

After a minute, he said, "I guess that settles it, doesn't it?"

"I guess it does."

Her face seemed blind, and she was like a ghost of Jody Gordon. Suddenly, Bill Roper knew that if he did not take the trail he had chosen now, he would never take it at all.

"You sure, Jody? You won't come?"

Again, she shook her head.

A long, loose end of Bill's rope was in his hand, though he never remembered taking it down. Hardly knowing what he did, he struck the spurs into the buckskin pony. The snap of the rope's end knocked a flying gout of fur from the rump of the black pack mule, and they were on the trail—the long trail, the dry trail, the trail of a hopeless war.

CHAPTER TEN

The men who rode with Roper saw Texas change.

They could not have foreseen the quick, unprecedented expansion of the cattle business, which would presently crowd not only Texas but every foot of the Great Plains. Nor could they have foreseen the almost immediate incursion of barbed wire, which was about to take unto itself everything that was worth fencing.

Yet they themselves, in no little part, forced the greatest change of all. They were fighting a thing they perhaps did not recognize as a national factor, but each, individually, had his own bitter motive. These men whom Roper now gathered about him hated a particular man, not only as lawless as themselves, but a man who was more than one man. Ben Thorpe was a thousand men. Operating under Cleve Tanner in the south, and Walk Lasham in the north, his innumerable retainers filamented the plains from the Rio Grande to the Big Horn. That Roper's men hated Ben Thorpe was no coincidence; Roper had picked men with personal grudges. Most of them had first been outlawed because they had not suited a single organization—the organization of Ben Thorpe.

Roper's wild bunch were assuredly lawless

men, but they were part of a West in which law was thin and obscure. The Rangers, youngsters with no limit of courage, had a list of men to get, and some of Roper's men were on that list. But Texas was big, and the Rangers were few, and most commonly absorbed with raids from Mexico, or with recalcitrant Indians still able to strike from Mexican fastnesses. Roper, sitting in the saddle, could look east, north, west, and know that as far as land reached, there was no cattle-barring fence. Here was the open range, as yet unbought by scrip or partitioned by barbed wire, an empire wrought by horse and gun. Southward lay the Rio Grande, the international barrier—a hazard to legal-minded men, a boon to men whose values did not attune with a distant, unenforceable law.

Into this vast open country, where every plant, animal, and rarely-seen man had its own particular sting, Roper now headed to cut the roots of Ben Thorpe's breeding grounds. The men who rode with him, as befitted men who lived by gun, rope, and rawhide whang, worked with the conditions that they found.

Up and down and across half of Texas, constantly in the saddle, Bill Roper threaded his new organization. Sometimes Dry Camp Pierce was with him; more often, he traveled alone. He was working with men of his own age now. The trail bosses and range foremen with whom he had been thrown heretofore had been older men, who had attained to responsibility by an experience that had its beginning with the founding of the Chisholm trail itself. But the wild bunch was something else.

These famous gunfighters and outlawed men whom Roper gathered were just youngsters, mostly. Some of them were true killers, some merely reckless kids who had gotten off on the wrong foot. All of them were badly wanted by what little law there was. Only Dry Camp Pierce, of them all, was much older than Bill himself. Because of his long and peculiar experience, he proved of infinite value, and yet at the same time was the most difficult to handle of all Roper's men.

One night in early June, Dry Camp Pierce and Bill Roper sat in the back room of a saloon, deep in Texas. This was at Whipper Forks—a place that is lost now. It consisted of only a store, a corral, and a bar. One other man was with them—an unnamed kid who was there because Dry Camp brought him there.

"It's funny," Pierce said, "I can't hardly place it. Here's you, a kid, and I guess you stand in the place of Dusty King. But—well, you know—Dusty King was the best friend I had in the world, but didn't ever seem like—"

"Didn't seem like he held with venting brands?" Bill Roper said.

“Look,” Dry Camp Pierce said, “I’ve stole cows until I could pave my way to hell with their hides. But—I don’t know—to steal cows for Dusty’s kid—”

Bill Roper’s teeth flashed clean in his grin. “Whose cows?”

“I’ve stole cows—”

“You’re going to steal cows that belong to me, now.”

“Figure you own these cows?”

“I’m Half of King-Gordon, now split. I’ve taken, out of King-Cordon, seven camps without cows. Now I’m claiming the cows that Thorpe took from Dusty King. And from some other men that we’re going to lend a hand to, pretty soon.”

“I suppose nobody’s got any better right—”

“To hell with that. I heard you can raise hell with the brand on a cow. Either I heard wrong—”

Bill Roper hadn’t heard wrong. Dry Camp Pierce—he was called that because he hated to camp too near to water—went to work for Bill Roper as he had never worked before, and thus the king of cow thieves, the brand changer extraordinary, for once aligned on the side of the law that was not.

“I got to have ten thousand advance,” Pierce said. “I’ll furnish my own boys, and I’ll turn cattle to you that don’t know their own mammies, or else you can slit my throat.”

“Won’t do,” Roper said.

"What's wrong, it won't do?"

"I've got to have ten camps the likes of you and your gang. You can spot them, or I can, I don't care. God damn it, this is no chickenyard cut!"

A slow, queer gleam came into Dry Camp's eyes. "You mean to back us, all the way through?"

"I'll back you while I can. After that—ride for the tall?" said Bill Roper without the least expression.

"Twenty-five thousand advance," said Pierce.

"Five thousand," Roper said. "You to get fifty per cent of what we can cash."

In the end, Pierce took fifteen thousand, Wells Fargo drafts, with Roper's word for a third split on proceeds of Dry Camp's wholesale scoops.

Ten rustlers' camps hooked into Thorpe-Tanner territory . . .

But Dry Camp also helped in other ways.

A hot, June dusk, five days after the meeting at Whipper Forks, found Bill Roper at the Dry Saddle Crossing, where he was to meet Lee Harnish. This meeting, too, was arranged by Dry Camp Pierce, though by this time, Pierce was far away.

Here ran the broad, many-channeled river, dividing two countries—a river whose split wanderings made two miles of intermittent shallows. At this border of a vast, imperceptibly rolling prairie stood a narrow string of adobe shacks. That was the Dry Saddle Crossing.

Two men—Bill Roper and Lee Harnish—sat in front of one of those abandoned shacks and tried to get together.

"I've always understood," Roper said, "that you were acquainted some, below the line."

Harnish's hard eyes studied Roper, and for a little while nothing could be heard except the mourning of doves in the willow scrub by the water. Next to Dry Camp Pierce, Lee Harnish was the oldest of those to join Roper at twenty-eight. He was tall and lank, sunbaked almost to the color of an Indian. His green eyes were curiously blank, impenetrable, and he liked to look his man in the eye with the peculiar fixity seen in the gaze of hawks.

"I've been down there some," he admitted. "I've made a few drives into Chihuahua, one drive to Mexico City."

"If you had a big wet herd run to you just below the line, would you know how to get rid of it?"

"I can't make out your hand," Harnish said. "King-Gordon never swung the long rope yet, that I heard of."

"I'm not King-Gordon now. My stunt is to smash Cleve Tanner, and I don't care what it costs."

"What's wrong with backing him into a shoot-out, if that's what you want?"

"That comes later. If I bust Tanner, I can bust Thorpe. But if Tanner is gunned before he's busted, Thorpe will take over in Texas, and the chance to break up his Texas layout will be gone."

"You ain't going to bust him by running off a few head of cattle. This river crossing is slow work, kid."

"I figure to cross five thousand head within the next three months," Roper told him.

"Five thousand head won't even scratch the hide of Thorpe and Tanner, son."

"I know that as well as you. What it will do is it'll draw Tanner to throw his warriors onto the border. That's what I want. Because by then I'll be working somewhere else."

"And you want me to take 'em on the other side—is that the idee?"

"I want three dollars a head, American gold, paid off as the cattle come out of the water . . ."

Roper's ways of gathering his wild bunch were diverse, as diverse as the saddle men he gathered. One way or another, picking up a man here, three more there, he got all he needed, and more.

But certain other things had to be done, in order that the wild bunch would have work to do, planned in such a way that something would be accomplished that would stay accomplished.

On a steamy afternoon early in July, Bill Roper sat in Fred Maxim's San Antonio law office. Maxim was an attorney who, some thought, had worked under a different name, somewhere before, but here, assuredly, he was in no one's pay.

"I'm not asking the likes of you what's what,"

Bill Roper said. "I want to know who actually owns range rights on the Graham stand."

The hard-bitten little man across the desk from Roper was still cagey. "When it comes to ousting a man from possession—"

"You know who 'ousted' Bob Graham and his family from possession. Cleve Tanner took over that outfit by main horse-and-gun power, without decent cause or reason. Everybody knows that. I'm asking you now—"

"Taylor and Graves are already doing everything that can be done to regain possession of Graham's outfit," Maxim said, smiling.

It was the smile that Roper liked. "Suppose I hold the Bob Graham lands, and Bob Graham's family are living on it. How long a delay can you give me in the courts? I mean, if Bob Graham, damn it, holds this land, will the Rangers interfere on behalf of Cleve Tanner?"

"Bob Graham hasn't got possession," Maxim said.

"Suppose he did have?"

"Never could happen. Ben Thorpe—"

"Shut up a minute," Roper said. "My time is measured out by the travel-trot of ponies, and God knows that's slow! I'm not asking you to put Graham back in possession of his range. I'm not asking you to save him from being put off again in the way he was before. What I want to know is, can you head off some cooked-up legal interference with Graham, after he's in possession again?"

Fred Maxim thought it over. "I can only promise you that I can cause considerable delay," he said.

"Months of delay?"

"Years, maybe. Have to see how it would work out."

"Start work," Roper decided. "I'll put up two thousand retainer. You go out and get an injunction protecting Bob Graham from molestation."

"But this assumes possession."

"I'll take care of that."

"I'd like to ask one question," Maxim said. "Why is it that you're suddenly so interested in Graham?"

"This isn't just Graham. If you can handle your end, this is only the first of many. There's going to be a lot of things straightened out between here and the Pecos, Fred."

"After all," Maxim said, "after all—maybe it's time!"

"You'll make a fight?"

"Providing you can show possession—I'll keep you clear until hell freezes."

"That's all I want . . ."

Still July, at Willow Creek—

A barren range of hills, sand hills, golden in the dawn, purple in the twilight, barren always.

Beneath them, what had been the Willow Creek camp of the old King-Gordon.

A mud and wattle bunkhouse. A futile stamping of ponies in the round corral beside the shallow river. In the bunkhouse nearest the river, five men were lounging around a little room.

"All right, you hard guys," Bill Roper said, "you know who told you to come here. Dry Camp Pierce told you to come here. Maybe he told you what you could look for here, huh?"

"Don't know as he did."

"All right. Maybe then you didn't figure on something you won't get. Because all I can promise you now is just your horses and your grub, my honey chil's!"

"We got horses. If we got horses, and a little lead, I guess we got grub . . ."

These four gunfighters who met Roper here were none of them older than Bill, yet each was famous as a killer in his own right. Of them all, Bill Roper alone had no name, no reputation. Yet, in respect for the name of Dusty King, they had come to hear him out.

Nate Liggett, a round-faced kid with eyelashes that looked as if they had been powdered with white dust, said, "Well, what seems to be your offer?"

"I guess you already know Bob Graham," Roper said. "You know how a warrior gang of Cleve Tanner's jumped down on him, on some thin excuse, and run him off his range. They even took over his house, his windmill, and his corrals. Now, I aim to hand back that range to Bob Graham. He's waiting in Bigspring for the word. Your part of the job is simple enough—you just go and take it away from the Tanner bunch."

"Simple, huh? Just how do you figure this simple trick is to be done?"

"How did the Tanner outfit get the range in the first place?"

"This sounds kind of rough," said Nate Liggett, with deceptive mildness. "Like something that would get the Rangers on our necks—very sure and quick!"

"A lawyer in San Antonio kept the Rangers off when Tanner jumped Graham. Now we've got another better lawyer in San Antonio to keep them off when Graham jumps Tanner. The only question is, who's got enough salt to grab that range—and then hang onto it?"

"And what do we get out of all this?"

"Graham takes over the outfit and runs it. You hang around and help him and see that he doesn't get run off again. For that, you get a half-interest in the outfit. You split it among you any way you see fit. I'll back Graham with cattle, and what other stuff he needs."

The others didn't say anything for a little while. It was Dave Shannon, huge-shouldered and blunt-faced, who finally spoke. "I'll tell you what it sounds like to me," he said, studying the curl of smoke from his cigarette. "Once there was a fellow watching driftwood come down the Mississippi River. He turns to another feller, and he says, 'You want a job? You fish this here driftwood out of the river, and I'll give you half of all you get.' "

Nate Liggett said, "It's a fact, Bill, I don't see where we come in for no advantage."

"You got a chance to do something here that will get you some place," Roper said good-humoredly. "First thing, you've got a chance to own some cattle in a way where you stand to get something out of it once in a while. Another thing, you get a certain amount of protection. Another thing, you're fixed up with a string of friendly camps, halfway across Texas. When you've got to move, there's always an established outfit you can head for, with fresh horses and whatever you need, waiting for you all the time."

"Been making out all right as it is, seems like," Red Miller said. He sprawled lazily, but he was squinting, his green eyes narrow, into the outer dark.

"If you're satisfied with this lone wolf stuff you've been pulling, I haven't got anything to offer you," Roper admitted. "But I'll tell you this—the boys that string with me now will see the day when they'll run Texas! And Cleve

Tanner, and Ben Thorpe, too, will be busted up and forgot!"

"It's a hefty order . . ."

"Maybe it is. This Graham business is a kind of experiment; it'll work if you make it work. But if it goes through okay—it's only the beginning, you hear me? You string with me a little while, and maybe, by God, we'll show a couple of people something . . ."

CHAPTER ELEVEN

Hot, dry days of early August—

As the first sun struck with a red heat across the plains, the Tanner men who held the Graham ranch were already saddling. All over Texas, cowmen were throwing together the last trail herds of the year. It was time for these Tanner men to roll their chuck wagons again, to round up the last of the trail-fit stock that remained in the herds which had belonged to Bob Graham.

At the crest of a rise, an unnamed cowboy lay flat to the ground, his rifle sighted through the short grass. Ultimately, inevitably, a rider came in line with his gunsight. It was the wrangler, loping out to bring his remuda in. Abruptly, his horse somersaulted as the rifle whacked from the hill, and the wrangler was afoot on the prairie.

Out from what had been the Graham corral, three riders swept through the dusty dawn, but they had hardly left the pole fences behind when six other riders confronted them, rising into their saddles like Comanches, out of the brush. The strangers closed in a semi-circle, unhurriedly, their carbines in their hands. In another minute or two, the three Tanner riders were grouped in a defensive knot, while from the semi-circle of the raiders, Nate Liggett jogged forward to talk it over.

"I don't think you want to go on," he said. "I don't even think you want to work for this outfit anymore."

Of the four gunfighters to whom Bill Roper had talked at Willow Creek, only Nat Liggett was here. Already, more work had been found for the others, and the four had split. They were far-scattered now, each gathering about him riders of his own whom he knew where to get.

But now the steel in the hands of Liggett's riders shone convincingly in the hot, dull light of first morning . . .

Two nights later, one hundred and fifty miles away—

With the approach of dusk, a peculiar light lay upon the valley of the Potreros; the sun went down in a copper welter, its light hanging on for a long time. In a reach of open grass, a herd of five hundred head bunched loosely—tame, heavy cattle, already well removed by breeding from the old, wild, longhorn strain. But they had not bunched voluntarily. They shuffled restlessly, watching the brush. Something was happening around them that they did not understand.

As the light failed, the figures of horsemen emerged from the brush, cutting mile-long shadows into the flat rays of sunset. The huge, heavy-shouldered man who signaled to his spread-out cowboys by turning his horse this way or that, in Indian horse language, was Dave Shannon.

They did not harass the cattle. Only, between sunset and the next daylight, no cow took a step other than in the direction of the Mexican border . . .

Dry-grass season; Texas scorched by the hot winds—

All across the southern ranges, a peculiar thing was happening. As word spread from twenty points of disturbance, certain of the older cattlemen began to sense that there was a curious, almost systematic order to what in itself seemed a widespread disruption. All over the Big Bend country, eastward almost to the well-settled Nueces, westward beyond the barren Pecos, northward to the fever line, was breaking a spotty wave of raids of an unparalleled boldness. Far apart, but almost simultaneously, hell had busted loose in a great number of places, covering more than half of Texas.

And presently it began to appear that the tough, notoriously trouble-making outfits under Cleve Tanner were not holding together as they always had before. For almost a decade, Ben Thorpe had been a law unto himself, and in Texas, Cleve Tanner had been the expression of that private law. For a long time, it had been supposed that to antagonize Cleve Tanner was to set against yourself the toughest and most unscrupulous range riders in Texas. But now it was beginning to appear that some of the toughest of them all were outside—and didn't want to get in. Here and there, men were beginning to desert the Tanner outfits—sometimes fired because they had failed, sometimes voluntarily deserting to the ranks of the raiders who were now almost openly punishing the Thorpe-Tanner holdings. Some of the first to be missed from the Tanner ranks were the very men upon whom Tanner had depended as the hard, cutting edge of his range-roughers . . .

Mid-August, in the season of driest heat—

Into the Potreros, by a little-used trail, a black-sombreroed horseman rode. He was a tested gunman, a proven man whose name was known and feared half the length of the Great Trail. Trouble-shooting for Cleve Tanner now, he was moving into the Potreros to find out what had gone wrong with some of Tanner's choicest herds. He had come fast, changing horses frequently, riding far into the night.

Loping down the almost invisible trail through the dark, his horse suddenly dropped from under him, headlong into nothingness. The pony might have stepped into a prairie dog hole—or it could have been the loop of a rope. But as the dazed rider struggled up, his mouth full of dirt, a rifle was prodding his belly, and a voice was saying, "Don't you think you might have took the wrong way?"

Mid-August still, at the edge of the vast quadrant of the sand hills—

A very quiet file of riders came in the middle of the night into a roundup camp on the range of the Cross-Bar-Cross. So cleverly they moved that they were between the wagons before anyone knew that something was wrong. The foreman—he had been one of Tanner's right-hand men almost since Tanner's beginnings—stood up in his blankets, suddenly as wide awake as a roused wolf.

Instantly a gun muzzle was in his armpit, and a soft voice was saying, "We're taking this camp over, Bud."

It was Windy Slater, most silent and usually most wary of all Bill Roper's lieutenants, who made that mistake. It was a mistake that brought quick disaster to raider and raided alike, for Slater had misjudged his man. A gun ripped out of its leather, and two guns spoke at once. In a moment, the camp was ablaze with the smashing reports of the short guns. Good brave cowboys, who didn't know what they were fighting for, but who spiked out gamely in the thin dark, dropped there on the Texas plain. A rumble of hoofs rose to a ground-shaking thunder as the held herd stampeded, later to break itself into a hundred bunches, lost in the sandy hills . . .

West Texas, far up the lonely Pecos—

One of Cleve Tanner's outfit bosses was talking to the Ranger stationed at Mustang Point.

"Such a damn' outburst of lawlessness has cut loose here as I never seen before," he said.

The ranger here was Val McDonald. He had gone out nineteen times in battle, sometimes against Mexicans, sometimes against the Comanches, and he had hunted white renegades galore.

"Awfully tough," he said in his own sympathetic way.

The foreman of the outfit that was busted up was fit to be tied. "I tell you, we're being stolen blind," he raved. "Not just a calf here and there, either—they take 'em in swoops and bunches. It's the boldest damn' thing I've ever seen. Even when there's no chance of getting clear with any cattle, they're game to stampede a cut herd that it's took weeks to round up, and scatter it from hell to—"

"This is one of Ben Thorpe's outfits, no?"

"Does that mean—"

"Well, what the hell, here? How many times has

Cleve Tanner passed out the word, 'The Rangers be damned'? He's put more obstructions in the way of things we was trying to do than any other man. Who was it had the legislature cut down our pay until we practically ride for nothing, and furnish all our own stuff?"

"The question here is whether we're going to have any law, or are we going to have—"

"From what I heard," McDonald said, "Cleve Tanner has let it be known that he's the biggest end of the law himself. Go talk to Cleve Tanner if you want law."

"My understanding is," the foreman argued, "that the Rangers are supposed to—"

"I'll move out and straighten up your little old range," McDonald said. "I'll be glad to. Just as soon as I get orders from headquarters. I'm waiting for them orders now!"

But the weeks rolled by, and headquarters was curiously still . . .

End of summer; a welcome end—

Cleve Tanner himself, *the* Cleve Tanner, who represented Ben Thorpe in the south, master of breeding grounds, the man who controlled the roots of all Ben Thorpe's plains organization, was talking to the United States Marshal at San Antonio.

"There hasn't been such a wave of outlawry

since the horse Indians was put down. Damnation, man! It's set us back ten years . . . I know what your policy has been. Your idea is to let us fight it out for ourselves, against Mexico, against the Indians, against all hell. But I tell you, this thing comes from inside. This thing might be something that I couldn't beat without help."

The United States Marshal at San Antonio smiled a little smile to himself and said, "Seems like this must be a terribly bad thing for you, Cleve?"

"I'm telling you—"

"Go ahead and tell me. You're a Ben Thorpe man, ain't you? A right leading Ben Thorpe man. Well—maybe I'll tell you a couple of things, someday . . ."

There was law in Texas, even in those days. But there was no such law as could stand against the combined renegades of the long trail, having a lawyer behind them who could delay forever in the courts, and a reckless expenditure of money, the source of which some suspected, but which was not definitely known.

CHAPTER TWELVE

With the fall, Lew Cordon, now in sole charge of the far-scattered cattle holdings he had shared with Dusty King, came to Texas to inspect the southern holdings of King-Gordon—the breeding ranges from which all the King-Gordon holdings drew their essential sustenance.

Reports kept coming to Bill Roper at his constantly shifting bases by way of the many riders who kept him in touch with his far-spread wild bunch. Nowadays, few things of consequence happened on the Texas ranges that he did not know. He was aware, almost to the day, when Jody Gordon and her father returned to Texas, and by report, he traced Lew Gordon's travels. Sometimes he grinned to himself, a little ironically, as he thought of what Gordon must be learning.

Inevitably, he knew that Jody was at the headquarters of the old Two-Circle, not far from Uvalde. The Two-Circle had been the original Gordon stand; from this camp had been driven the first trail herd that Dusty King had pushed north. It was a different outfit now than it had been then, for today it was King-Gordon's main headquarters in Texas. Here, as at Ogallala, Gordon had seen to it that a suitable house had been put up, of painted wood. Except that here, instead of the tall jig-sawed towers Lew Gordon had designed for Ogallala, the house was simple and rambling, based on the first little home in which Jody had been born.

Roper knew that she was there. Yet the fall dragged on, and November passed into December before he went to see her.

The northers were sweeping the Texas plains as Christmas drew near—bitter winds that rushed across a thousand miles without obstruction, gathering a blasting force. The wild bunch was as good as holed up, as there was little they could do. Roper's time now was spent in riding from one to another of those ranches upon which he had rehabilitated the men who had owned them before Cleve Tanner had swallowed them up. To hold his organization steady through the winter months was about all that he could accomplish. He hadn't done all he had hoped to do before winter closed—not half of what he had hoped to do. Now, he could only hang on and plan for the action that spring would bring.

He had told himself that there was no use in his going to see Jody Gordon, but in the end, of course, he went.

He rode up to the Two-Circle ranch house in late afternoon of a cold December day. The sky was low and heavy, and the bitter norther had brought a scud of hard snow a long way to throw it in his face. Night was closing down two hours early, so that it was almost dark as he approached. There were ponies in the corrals, and threads of smoke trailed from the chimneys, but the place looked so tightly shut up that he could have readily believed that no one was there—certainly no one who wanted to see him now.

He pulled up his horse a few yards from the kitchen gallery, then sat there looking at the house, his sheepskin hunched about his throat. Even now, having come this far, he almost made up his mind to go away.

Then Jody Gordon stepped out on the gallery in a whippy woolen dress and stood estimating the uninvited horseman through the dusk. Something like the strike of a buffalo lance went through Bill Roper. It had been so long since he had seen that one slim little figure that could so change everything under the sky for him.

A split pole fence separated them, and after a moment, she came across the few yards of space, leaning sideways against the bitter wind, and stood gripping a bar of the fence as she peered up into his face.

"I knew it was you," she said.

"Child," said Bill Roper, "you get back in that house. You'll freeze!"

"Then you put up your horse and come in."

"Is your father here?"

"He's in San Antonio."

"I don't think he'd want me here, Jody."

"Lew Gordon has never turned away any rider without a cup of coffee, not yet."

He gave in then and stepped down, but when she tried to insist that he put his pony in the barn, a fragment of an old song went through his head—

"Most horses ain't hungry,
They won't eat your hay—"

"I'll only be here about a minute." Stubbornly, he tied his horse to the fence and followed her into the house.

The fire in the big wood range made the room a dazzling contrast to the cold sweep of the prairie. He threw his coat open, but he did not take it off.

"How have you been?" he asked.

"I've been all right. You?"

"I've been all right."

Then a silence dropped between them, there in the long dusky kitchen of the ranch house; such an empty, unusable silence as he had never seen between them before.

"Of course," Jody said, "we keep hearing about you."

"That's too bad. I expect you wouldn't be hearing anything good."

"No."

Silence again. He didn't know why he had

come; there wasn't anything he could say. He stood by the stove, his eyes brooding on the iron. Deep in the pockets of his coat, there was a trembling in his slack fingers, not caused by cold. It was a strange and uncomfortable thing to be so near this girl again, and yet to be so far away.

"Still," Jody said, "you seem to be getting done what you set out to do."

"Sometimes it looks like I'm not even doing that."

"You've made a name," she told him. "Nothing definite yet, but I guess it will be definite soon enough. People are beginning to piece things together and add up two and two. Cowmen that are wise know the truth, I guess."

"What truth?"

"If you haven't accomplished anything else, you've astonished my father. He's said himself, over and over, he wouldn't have supposed it could be done. No question that Cleve Tanner is shaken; he's shaken clear down to his roots. Nobody knows what's what anymore, or what will happen. People who thought a year ago that Cleve Tanner was invincible—they're saying now that he's coming to the end of his string, and that if this thing goes on, Tanner will be through."

"What else do they say?"

"They're saying that the worst renegades of the trail are working together, for the first time—the killers, the men who don't care if they live or die. They say they have money behind them now, and that even Cleve Tanner, with all his string of outfits, can't stand up against the everlasting raiding, and stampeding, and mysterious loss of cattle. They say he's lost twenty outfits, just because he couldn't spare the gunmen to hold the range."

"Eleven outfits," Roper said.

"Then it was really you?"

"Those eleven outfits they speak of—those were outfits roughed away from little lonely men, on pretenses that hadn't any justice or any true law. Those outfits are back with their owners now."

"But—you admit your wild bunch is behind all this?"

"Call it that if you want to. I guess there isn't anybody who knows as well as you do what I'm trying to do."

She was looking at him in an odd way. Her face was a pale oval, and her eyes looked curiously dark in the failing light. She said in a dead voice, "I never believed it . . . I couldn't believe it—until now."

"Didn't I tell you about it? I told you about it before I began. I set out to break Cleve Tanner, and by God, he'll be broken—if I live."

"You know Cleve Tanner has put up five thousand dollars for your arrest?"

Bill Roper chuckled crazily. "All right. I'll put

up ten thousand for his arrest. There isn't going to be any arrest, and he knows that, too."

"I can't believe it," she kept saying over and over. "I can't believe it even yet."

"You can't believe what?"

"That you're an outlaw—a wild bunch boss—thrown in with the ugliest killers this range has ever seen, or any range—"

He said ironically, "Don't hardly see how I could use second-rate men."

"Reports have come in," Jody said wonderingly, "from over eight hundred miles of country. They're beginning to call it a rustlers' war, a final showdown between the wild bunch and lawful men. And you—"

"What about me?"

"Oh, Billy, it's unbearable! That you—you've turned yourself into the festering point of all that struggle, and hate, and lawless gunning—"

He had to grin at that, unhappy as he was. "Didn't realize I was festering," he said.

"You had everything," she said, "and you threw it away . . ."

He had only heard her say that once before, but, in memory, he had heard it so often since that her words had the ring of a familiar song.

It was Bill Roper who rebelled this time. "I'm sorry," he said.

Her voice lashed out at him. "You're sorry for what?"

"I'm sorry that we can't ever see things the same. I started out to get Cleve Tanner, and I'll get him, so help me God. After Tanner, Walk Lasham, and after Walk Lasham, Ben Thorpe. But when it comes to saying I had everything before I started in, I guess maybe that isn't so,"

Jody said hotly, "There wasn't one thing in all the world you didn't have—or couldn't have had—before you chose this crazy way!"

"I didn't have you," he told her. "If I had had you, I guess I would have you yet. Things don't shift and change so easy as that—not in the part of the world I know."

He was pulling on his gloves now, buttoning his sheepskin coat. In what was left of the light, the shadows lay heavy upon his face. As he stood there, he could have been Dusty King himself—the man who had broken a hundred long and weary trails, except that Dusty King had perhaps never looked so old.

Her voice came to him as if from a distance. "And when you're through," she said—"what are you going to have left?"

"Far as I know," Bill Roper said, "I'm not going to have anything left. God knows I've got very little left now." He was glad she didn't know how his resources had dwindled, how close to the end he really stood.

Her voice rose sharply. "Can't you see there's no hope in this ghastly thing? Thorpe's grip is unbreakable. A hundred men—older and wiser than you'll ever be!—they've gone against him, over and over again, and he smashed them all."

"Maybe," he said, "there had to be somebody who was willing to cut loose—to the last dollar, to the last pony, to the last round of lead. Maybe it might turn out, after all, that this range was waiting for somebody who was willing to throw everything away."

She came close to him, and her words came through her teeth. "It's your very life you're throwing away!"

Perhaps he misunderstood her then, for he grinned. "Maybe," he said, "that would be the least I could lose, the very least of all . . ."

CHAPTER THIRTEEN

The winter dragged out slowly. It was not marked by the interminable tedium of a three months' trail drive, for here was action, in the continual flux and flow of a struggle which had attained the proportions of a widespread war. But in other ways, it carried punishment enough.

Roper's plans, bold as they were, had been well laid. He had perceived from the first that success or failure depended upon whether or not he could make his war with Tanner self-sustaining. To gnaw away at the Tanner herds was one thing; to turn their captures into cash was altogether another. Roper had hoped that he could initiate his own drives to the north, but he had found this out of the question. On the other hand, the trail drivers had found themselves so vulnerable that none of them wanted to buy cattle of questionable ownership.

The Thorpe-Tanner organization did not have this problem; they took what they wanted and drove what they wanted by means of their own trail outfits. But Roper could now only dispose of cattle for the trail through ranchers known to be scrupulous and established men.

This was the strategic purpose behind Roper's rehabilitation of the eleven outfits which Tanner had originally seized, and which Roper had now put back into the hands of their proper owners. These re-established ranchers had not only the sympathy but the respect of everyone who knew anything about Texas cattle. Through these men, Roper now had a safe and sure outlet for the cattle recovered by Dry Camp's experts, while the gunfighters under such men as Nate Liggett, Tex Daniels, and Hat Crick Tommy supplied a much-needed protection until they could get on their feet.

But this method, promising as it was, was slow. Of necessity, the men whom Roper backed were cowmen without assets other than their disputed claim to their ground. Sometimes by mortgage loans, but principally by silent partnerships, Roper had now obtained interests in nearly a dozen outfits. They should have been thriving outfits. But Roper found his money draining away with unforeseen swiftness, without hope of any financial return until the trail should open in the spring. Only the Mexican border operations, which depended upon Lee Harnish, continued to show a thin trickle of income through the winter months. As spring approached, Roper found himself near the end of his string.

Early in February, Shoshone Wilce came south seeking Bill Roper and found him at the Pot Hook ranch.

Shoshone Wilce was a grim-mouthed, bottle-nosed little man. His small eyes had a persistent twinkle, and usually the dry twist of his humor enabled him to ingratiate himself among men who ordinarily would not have tolerated his impudence. He was especially interesting to Bill Roper because of his notable faculty for obtaining news of a type hard to get at.

All winter, Shoshone Wilce had been traveling in Bill Roper's pay, and Roper had heard from him seldom.

"I thought they must have hung you," Roper said.

"No, but they did give me a hell of a bad cold."

"Find out anything?"

Shoshone Wilce rubbed his badly shaved chin with horny fingers. "I don't know as you're going to like this so very good, Bill."

"Let's have the bad news first—I eat it up."

"God knows there's enough of it. There ain't any other kind to be had. What do you want to know first?"

"How's Thorpe making out up above?"

"I've been all over their short grass ranges," Shoshone said. "He's holding enough cattle, between the fever line and the Canadian River alone, to last him from here out, even if he never gets hold of any more."

"How many thousand head do you think he'll have to have from Cleve Tanner?"

"I can't see he'll need any from Cleve Tanner. I

saw him in Dodge City. He was throwing money around with a shovel in each hand. You know what I think? I think he can go away and forget Tanner and write everything he has in Texas right off the books, and never know the difference, by God!"

Roper locked his hands behind his head and stared at the ceiling. Sometimes it seemed to him that trying to break Tanner was like trying to empty the Rio Grande with a hand dipper. The apparently unbounded resources of Ben Thorpe in the middle country and in the north, out of reach of the south Texas war, made up a vast reservoir which Tanner could draw on without limit.

"How is Tanner himself making out?"

"Bill, I've been all up and down the north and east part of Texas, and I can't see where we've accomplished a damned thing."

"You don't know what you're talking about!"

"You know what I think?" Wilce persisted. "I think there's too many cattle in this country nowadays. I think there's more cattle in this country than the world has any use for. I don't think you can bother any man anymore, just by fooling with his cattle."

"Never mind what you think. Let's have what you know."

"I nosed around and tried to find out what promises Tanner's been making for cattle on spring deliveries. I didn't learn everything. Nobody learns everything. But I got enough to total up."

Shoshone Wilce hesitated and didn't say any more until he had gotten a cigarette rolled. In the middle of rolling his cigarette, he went into a coughing fit and spilled the tobacco, so that he had to start over again.

"Bill," he said at last, "Cleve Tanner's going to drive more cattle this year than he's ever drove before. In just one bunch alone, he aims to deliver fifteen thousand head on the banks of the Red!"

"He's crazy!" Roper shouted. "He can't do it—damn it, it's impossible!"

"Well—he thinks he can. He knows his cattle counts better than me. But—I've been all up and down this country, and I don't see but what he can."

Bill Roper returned to studying the peeled poles that supported the roof, his face expressionless, his gray eyes opaque. He heard Shoshone say, "I don't believe we've even touched Cleve Tanner. I don't believe we've scratched his hide at all."

"Well, anyway," Roper said, "the border gangs are going good. We'll go on with it, and keep going on . . ."

"Bill," Shoshone said, "how long can you go on, the way it's costing you now?"

"Not much farther, I guess."

"You going to have to quit?"

Roper shook his head. “I’ll never quit now, Shoshone, I can’t quit. While I’ve got one rider left with me, or no riders, I’ll still be working on Cleve Tanner. But I think we’re going to beat him, Wilce. After all, the border gangs—we can count on them.”

Roper continued to count on his border gangs for two weeks more. Then, in the middle of February, he learned that Lee Harnish was through.

The first word of difficulty came when Dave Shannon pushed a little bunch of seven hundred head through the river at Mudcat Turn and found no vaqueros waiting on the other side. Shannon waited three days before he was forced to turn the cattle free and ride.

The complete news of what had happened never really came. What Roper learned came in bit by bit, by way of random riders who had talked with a vaquero here, another there.

Lee Harnish had been pressing south with a herd of twelve hundred head. He was two days into Mexico and supposed that he was clear; he had never had much trouble, once he was well below the line. But now, one moonless night, a band reported as of at least sixty men struck from no place, scattering the herd, and blazing down on Harnish’s riders almost before they could take to the saddle. There had been a sharp running fight as Harnish and his half-dozen boys took to the brush and the hills. Unsatisfied with seizure of the herd, the unknown band had spent three days trying to hunt down Harnish's riders.

Lee Harnish himself, wounded in the first skirmish, had had a hard time getting clear. It was not known whether or not all of his riders were elsewhere accounted for.

After an elapse of several weeks, an Indian-faced vaquero came hunting Bill Roper. He carried a written message from Lee Harnish:

> "This thing is finished up. Don't let anybody tell you it was Cleve Tanners men busted into us. What he's done, this Tanner has put some bunches of Mex renegades up to landing on us, they work with the Yakis, and his Indian scouts have spotted where we make our crossings. Seems like there's at least a dozen bands of them haven't got anything else to do but lay watching those crossings and wait us out.
>
> "About half of them is carrying new American guns and plenty ammunition. They got our hide nailed to the fence all right and we are through."

It was a long time before Roper saw Lee Harnish again. He did not accept Harnish's statements off-hand, but when he had conferred with Dave Shannon and others of the border men in whom he believed, he was forced to accede that the border-running phase of the attack on Tanner was done.

As February drew to a close, the big herds were once more being thrown together for the trail. From the eleven rehabilitated outfits in which Roper was now a silent partner, a little trickle of trail cattle began to move toward the gathering grounds on the Red. The income from these sales helped a little, but the proceeds were principally absorbed by debts incurred on behalf of the individual ranches. The improvement in his situation for which Roper had hoped did not come.

It was deep into March when Tex Long quit.

Sun, wind, and sleet had turned Tex Long's face a red-gold brown, but without wrinkles. The smooth, satiny leather of his face seemed unscarred, except for that betraying dark color that bespoke the long rider. Nobody ever questioned Tex Long's guts—Bill Roper did not do so now.

"Look," Tex Long said, "look." He did not talk easily; whatever he said was matter-of-fact, even now. "I got to pull out of this game."

Bill Roper looked at him, without expression. "All right. How much you figure I owe you?"

Tex smiled. "Nothing."

A very rare flush of anger came into Bill Roper's face. "Tex, what's the matter with you?"

"You want to know what's the matter with me? I'll tell you what's the matter with me. You noticed I used very few boys?"

"Yeah, I noticed that."

Tex Long could have had six riders, or eight, or fifty—only three men rode with him. But they did what they started out to do.

"When I go in with my boys, I go in because I know we got the other side beat."

Bill Roper said with asperity, "When you don't 'have the other side beat' I'll get somebody else."

"This," said Tex Long gently, "is the time for you to get somebody else."

"I'd sure like to know what's busted."

"Goin' yellow," Long grinned.

"No," Roper answered. "No, Tex."

"I'm sorry, Bill. I hate Cleve Tanner like you do. But I'll be damned if I'll take good fast-shooting boys into their death."

"God damn it, I told you, you never rode with enough men!"

Tex Long said, almost sleepily, "I took with me boys I could count on, Bill."

"Let's see—Bill Roper said—"what was it I asked you to do—"

"You said I was to take back the Bert Johnson ranch."

"And you can't do it, huh?"

"No, I can't do it."

"In God's name, Tex—"

Tex Long made a quick, futile gesture with his hands. "We used to be able to jump down on them. We can't do that now. The Bert Johnson place is studded with rifles until a man can't take a step. Every place you'll find out it's the same. There isn't going to be anything more we can do. We went good for a while. But they got organized, now. We're through."

"Speak for yourself," Bill Roper said.

"I'm speaking for myself."

"And you want how much?"

"Nothing, I told you . . ."

Tex Long was only one of Bill Roper's picked gunfighters, but he was one of the best. As March drew on, Roper lost four more. He could have had men who would have gone in shooting, gone in to kill or to die, but that was not his game. He could not bring himself to a warfare of guns against guns. He was fighting a thing; he was not fighting nameless, hired cowboys who would fight for their brand, because cowboys were what they were.

Into the Big Bend, into the valley of the Nueces, Cleve Tanner had flooded such a power of gunfighters as Bill Roper would not have believed. He had supposed that he could outplace and outsmart Tanner's warrior outfits. But now his raiding forces met everywhere a stubborn resistance.

Roper had discounted the quit of Tex Long,

but now other news was coming in. The Graham outfit—the first of all those that the Roper men had taken—was again in the hands of Cleve Tanner, and Nate Liggett, assigned to protect Graham, had headed for the tall without even a report. Hat Crick Tommy was three weeks missing. The Davis outfit, left under his protection, had gone the way of all loose outfits, and Tanner's cowboys rode the range.

Dry Camp Pierce was almost the last to come in—of those who came in at all.

Pierce rode into the Pot Hook Camp early in April. He was the same, small, wiry man he always had been—his eyes watery, his jaws poorly shaven. He rallied a little, in his old cocky way, as he said to Bill, "How's it going?"

But it was apparent to Bill Roper that even this man, much older than himself, seemed older than he had ever seen him before.

"I'm pretty near ashamed," Dry Camp said, "to ask you for any more money now."

"Go ahead and be ashamed," Roper said, grinning his clean grin. "I hope it pretty near kills you. Because you know as well as I do, there's no money here."

"I was scared of that."

"In the name of Christ, Dry Camp," Roper said, "the first money that comes to me, that money belongs to you. If you don't think I'm good for it—"

Dry Camp Pierce shot straight up on his heels, and his voice rose. "God damn you—don't I tell you—"

Bill Roper—the kid, the youngster who had hardly been born when Dry Camp first haunted the trails—Bill Roper sat motionless, his face a lamp-lit mask. "Then what do you want?"

"Bill—it's only—it's only—"

"Well, spit it out!"

"Bill, I can't carry these camps no more. God knows we strung with you while we could. We've et beef, beef without salt or flour, we've et bobcat meat. But Bill, there's no lead in our guns, and there's no patches in our pants, and it's time I got to let the boys go, to make out any way they can."

Roper laughed in his face. "Your boys getting too good to eat beef?"

Pierce angered. "You tell me and my bunch—"

Bill Roper looked older than Dusty King had ever looked, his face like granite, with hard lines cut into it by the weather.

"Okay," he said. "I understand how you feel, Dry Camp."

Dry Camp's anger was gone as quickly as it had come. "Bill," he said pleadingly, "it's only—it's only—"

"It's only that you've had a lot of men out working for us," Bill Roper said more reasonably.

"Near fifty men," Dry Camp said, "and I swear

I couldn't have held them, if it hadn't've been for—for—"

"If it hadn't been for Dusty King," Bill said.

Pierce was silent.

"How many you got working now?"

Dry Camp Pierce hesitated.

"Not a damned man," Bill Roper said.

"Bill, it's been the shiningest fight I've ever seen in all my days, I don't blame nobody but myself."

"What do you mean by that?"

"You was only a kid, Bill—the kid that Dusty left. I never told you this before. I'll tell you now. I was with Dusty King that time he picked you up."

"It seems funny," Roper said, "you never told me that."

"I don't know why I never. I was with Dusty King that first drive up from Uvalde. Tom—your father—he was trying the old way to Sedalia. Dusty figured something was wrong. We rode over and cut into Tom's trail. I was with Dusty when he rode into your father's wrecked camp. I seen it all. I saw—but let that go. I was there when Dusty King dropped down on one knee, and kind of held out his arms to the buckbrush—and you ran out, a little kid . . ."

"And now you quit Dusty King," Bill Roper said.

"Look you here," Dry Camp said. "I've strung

with you when I wouldn't have strung with any other man, let alone an upstart kid. I'll say this for you, by God—you've made a game fight. But kid, take my word for it—they're too big, and they're too strong."

"You think so?" Bill Roper said.

"I know so. I don't know what you had, made men like Lee Harnish and Dave Shannon and Nate Liggett throw in with you, but they did—the damnedest wild bunch Texas ever seen. Half the renegades of the Long Trail, and your part of King-Gordon, has gone into beating Cleve Tanner. And where are we now?"

"Well?"

"We aren't any place! Damn it, kid, I tell you we're beat, and we're long beat!"

"And I say we've only begun!" Bill Roper thundered.

"You're broke," Dry Camp Pierce said, "and everything you've tried is busted. But I swear to God, if you can show me one place more we can hit, I'll swing along."

"I can't show you anything," Roper admitted. "How can I show you anything when I can't pay you anything?"

April melted into May, and Roper had nothing to fight with anymore. Those units of his wild bunch that had not quit had not been heard from at all, and he knew already that the ones he had not heard from were the ones who had completely failed. Cleve Tanner prospered, seemingly, and all was well with Ben Thorpe.

Bill Roper waited at the Pot Hook now, trying to think of some way that he had missed. His broad campaign had been effective in one thing only: he could no longer expect anything from Lew Gordon. Roper's fantastic foray against Tanner had made itself felt on such a widespread front as to have earned the name of a Rustlers' War; King-Gordon denied him, and Lew Gordon expressedly would advance nothing more against Dusty King's share of the partnership which had been broken by death . . .

Dry Camp Pierce still loafed at the Pot Hook, dejected, hopeless. No one knew what he was waiting for. Roper never heard from the rest of them now. In spite of everything that Maxim could do, the Rangers were on the loose. The wild bunch that had threatened to dominate Texas was broken and split, scattered far and wide, every man for himself. Day and night, a saddle pony waited beside the door of the bunkhouse in which Roper slept . . .

Now, unexpectedly, came Shoshone Wilce.

Roper had not seen him since that first dark, discouraging news that Shoshone Wilce had brought eight weeks before.

Nothing could tell more of Roper's present position than this: as Shoshone Wilce rode up, Bill Roper already had his gun in his hand,

and the other hand upon the bridle rein of his pony.

Shoshone Wilce almost tumbled into Bill Roper's arms. He grabbed Bill by both lapels of the black, town-going coat that Roper always wore when he was about to travel a long way. Shoshone's bottle-nose gleamed and quivered, and his eyes were like shoe buttons.

"It's done! He's bust—he's split—he's cracked—"

"What the hell are you talking about?"

"Cleve Tanner, by God! I tell you, he's gone to hell!"

Suddenly, Bill Roper turned into the unaccountable kid that his years justified. Like a man suddenly coming alive, he took Shoshone by the throat, shook him as if he had weighed no more than a cat. His teeth showed bare and set.

He said, "Shoshone—you fool with me—"

Shoshone cried out through the grip on his throat, "I tell you, Cleve Tanner—"

He couldn't say any more, and now Bill Roper came to himself and let go of Shoshone so abruptly that the little man almost dropped in his tracks.

"Come in," he said unsteadily, "come in and have a cup of coffee, and set."

"Listen, damn your soul, I tell you Cleve Tanner is through!"

Bill Roper was cool again, now. "What makes you think so?"

"He failed his delivery at the Red. Where he was supposed to bring up fifteen thousand head, a little handful of punchers showed up with a few hundred. He can't round his cattle—if he's got any cattle—and he can't make delivery at the Red!"

Bill Roper walked a little way off from Shoshone Wilce, and he leaned against the butt ends of the poles that formed a corner of the corral. He said, "I ought to have known it. There isn't the outfit nor the string of outfits, in all the plains, that can stand up against the punishing Cleve Tanner took . . ."

"We didn't believe you," Shoshone Wilce babbled on. "We all said it couldn't be done. But by Christ, we've done it! All over Texas, Tanner's notes are being called, as the word spreads. Wells Fargo refuses to honor his signature for a dime. They say now that Ben Thorpe won't back Tanner—Thorpe denies him, and the Tanner holdings are being closed up and sold out—"

"I ought to have known," Bill Roper said again, "I did know, only, they all quit me, and took to the tall, and talked me out of it . . ."

Shoshone Wilce seemed to realize what had happened better than Bill Roper was able. After all, Shoshone was the one who had been and seen.

"He's beat, and he's whipped, and he's wiped out, and he's through!" Shoshone exulted.

"You sure?" Roper asked, looking up from the ground again.

"Am I sure? You think I'd risk my damn throat coming here to tell you something like this, if I didn't know for sure?"

"No," Roper admitted. "I guess not."

"It's all over," Shoshone tried to tell him. "Can't you realize it, man?"

"No," Roper said.

CHAPTER FOURTEEN

Strolling, easy-going, but somehow reluctant, Bill Roper walked the streets of Tascosa, between the false-fronted wooden buildings that lined the hoof-stirred dust.

Sooner or later, he knew, Cleve Tanner would appear upon this one main street. But as the days dragged by and Tanner did not come, Roper could not have said whether he was anxious to get the meeting over with or whether he would have put it off if he could. The word that Shoshone Wilce had brought to the Pot Hook was on everybody's tongue now. All Texas seemed to know that Ben Thorpe had refused to pull Cleve Tanner out of the hole—had sacrificed his own interests in Texas, to let Tanner take the full brunt of the disaster. And everybody knew that Tanner was on the warpath, determined to seek out Bill Roper. It was said that Tanner's only remaining interest was to bring down the youngster who had cut Texas from under him.

Yet ten days passed before Cleve Tanner came.

It was eleven o'clock on a sunny Saturday morning when Dry Camp Pierce brought Bill the word.

"Well, kid, he's here. You were right again—

you won't have to hunt him out. He's looking for you. All you have to do is wait."

"Where is he now?"

"In some bar, a block up the street. He's walking from bar to bar, asking if you've been seen. You might as well wait for him here."

"No," Roper said. "I'll walk out and meet him, I think."

"Every man to his own way. First, better have a drink."

Bill Roper stood leaning on the bar, his fingers twirling the whiskey glass the bartender set out. This moment was the one he had worked toward, constantly and insistently, ever since the killing of Dusty King. He had thrown everything he had into the breaking of Cleve Tanner, as a necessary preliminary to rubbing him out, and canceling the first of the three who had put Dusty under the prairie. Five minutes more would finish forever the job he had worked on unflaggingly for more than a year.

Yet now that he faced it, Roper felt no sense of triumph or success. He knew he was going to go through with what was ahead, but he found now that he hated it more than anything he had ever gone against. His only sense of anticipation was one of bitter distaste.

Dry Camp peered up into his face. "Kid, you look sick!"

"I don't feel real happy," Roper admitted.

"You shaky, kid?"

Roper held out his right hand, fingers extended. They showed no tremor.

"Steady as a rock," Dry Camp commented. "Don't worry. You'll come through."

"I know I will."

"Draw deliberate and slow," Pierce counseled. "Take your time,—don't hurry, whatever you do. But don't waste any time, either. Fast and smooth—"

"I get you," Roper said with a flicker of a grin. "Take my time, but be quick about it. Move plenty slow, but fast as hell. All right, Dry Camp!"

He gave the butt of his gun a hitch to make sure it was loose in its leather, then he spun the whiskey away from him untasted and walked out.

Dry Camp Pierce looked at the full glass and exchanged a worried glance with the bartender. Then he followed Bill.

"Walk in the middle of the street," he told Bill as he caught up. "There ain't so much chance of killing some fool that sticks his head out of a door to see the excitement."

"Okay." Roper stepped into the dust, between tire-tied cow ponies, and walked down the middle. "I'll be seeing you."

"Oh, I'll get out of the way. When it's time."

Dry Camp kept blinking his eyes in the bright light, as if they were dry. His lids looked tight, and there were white patches at the corners of his mouth. When he tried to spit, he could not.

"Don't give him too much of a break, kid. He's awful bad. But you'll get him, all right," he added hastily.

Little groups of punchers that stood on the board sidewalks drew back close to the building, or into doorways. The whole street seemed to become motionless and very quiet. A man ran out of a saloon, untied a beautiful three-quarters-bred mare, and led her into the saloon. She reared at the doorway, but he got her in. Dry Camp laughed. "Get your toys in, children! Going to rain lead!" His face looked feverish.

Half a block ahead, another man stepped into the street and walked toward Bill. Before his face could be seen in the black shadow under his hat, Bill Roper knew by the set of the broad shoulders, by the rolling swing of his stride, that it was Cleve.

"Here he comes," Dry Camp said unnecessarily.

" 'Bye, Dry Camp."

"Good luck, kid." Dry Camp dropped away from Roper's elbow and was instantly out of Bill's thoughts.

The moments during which the two men walked toward each other drew out interminably. Their eyes were upon each other's faces now. Bill could see that Cleve Tanner looked happy, almost gay, as if this was the first good thing that had happened to him for a long time. A little nearer, and it could be seen that there was a touch of craziness in his eyes, in his half grin.

At twenty paces, Tanner suddenly spoke. "Draw, kid, if you've got the guts!"

"Draw yourself," Roper said.

At twelve paces, Cleve Tanner drew. To observers, the men seemed so close together that it was impossible that either of them should live. Tanner's gun spoke five times, fast, faster than most men could slip the hammer. Nobody knew where the first four shots went, but the fifth shot was easy to place, for it blew a hole in the street as Tanner's gun stubbed into the dust.

Bill Roper holstered his own smoking forty-four. He had fired twice.

Dry Camp Pierce was at his elbow again. "Here's the horses. It's time to ride. By God, I knew you could take him, kid."

Roper was feeling deathly sick.

CHAPTER FIFTEEN

It was well into the summer as Bill Roper once more rode south out of Ogallala toward the pile of stones that marked the grave of Dusty King. Jody Gordon rode with him. In the few days he had stopped over in Ogallala, he had hardly seen her at all. At first, she had refused to ride with him today, but at the last moment, as if on an impulse, she had changed her mind.

A hot summer wind was sweeping across the prairies, a dry and shriveling wind that parched the needle grass, cracked the lips of riders, and turned tempers short and irritable. It seemed to Roper that Jody Gordon looked sad and lifeless. She rode with her face set straight ahead. The loose ends of her soft hair, whipping in that hot wind, kept striking across her cheeks like tiny whips, but she didn't seem to notice or care.

Roper, studying her sidelong, thought that Jody seemed to have aged several years in one. Impossible now to find any trace of the irrepressible, upwelling laughter that had been so characteristic of her a year before. Her eyes were unlit and a little tired-looking. Her mouth was expressionless except for a faint droop at the corners, which suggested—perhaps resignation, perhaps a hidden bitterness.

She didn't have much to say, but finally, she asked him, "What did my father decide?"

"He says now that I'll never have another penny out of Dusty King's share until—until he's able to dictate to me what I'm going to do with it . . . Or that's what it amounts to."

"You mean, until you quit this ghastly wild bunch stuff?"

"That's it. But he goes farther than that now. He says now that if I go any further, he's through with me forever. But I guess you knew that already, didn't you?"

"It's about what I expected," Jody said.

"About what you wanted him to do, too, I should think."

"I can't see that it mattered, either way. Whatever we—whatever he thought or did, you'd go on just the same. You're the hardest man I've ever known. Nothing could possibly change you; I can see that now. I think you don't care about anything or anybody in the world, except this one terrible purpose."

"It's true I have to go on."

"Did you quarrel with my father?"

"No. He said some kind of bitter things, but I didn't say anything. I asked for certain things—five camps in Montana, mainly. Of course, that was a waste of breath."

"I suppose," Jody said, "you could force an accounting through the courts."

"I wouldn't do that. Wouldn't feel I could."

"But you'll go on, and throw yourself against Walk Lasham in Montana?"

"Yes, I have to go on."

"But how?"

"I don't know how, yet," he admitted.

"With your wild bunch broken up and scattered, and without any money, or any way to get any, you'll still try to break Walk Lasham."

"I'll have to find ways."

They were silent after that, and presently they sat, almost stirrup to stirrup, but somehow infinitely far apart, looking down at the stacked boulders from which rose the wooden cross that Bill Roper had made, nearly a year and a half ago.

After a few moments, Bill Roper stepped down and replaced a boulder that had rolled to the ground. As he did so, something between the stones caught his eye. Leaning closer, he saw that some little handfuls of Indian paintbrush had been put here, tucked down in the crevices so that they were secure from the hot clawing of the wind. It was late in the season for prairie flowers. Whoever had gathered them must have ridden a long way to find the few survivors.

Bill said to Jody, "You put flowers here?"

"Sometimes."

He looked at her hard. He thought her lips were trembling, and for a moment, he hoped that the barriers behind her eyes were about to dissolve, so that she would be a little closer to him again, if only for a little while. But she bit her lips, and her eyes as she returned his gaze were bleak, empty.

He turned away, grim with a sense of illimitable loss. But he had chosen his way, and he had no thought of turning back.

For a little while, he stood looking at the cross which he had made of railroad ties. He said, half aloud—"One down. Dusty . . ."

"I suppose," Jody said, "you'll be cutting a notch on the handle of your gun, now."

He was surprised to hear her say that. He had no way of knowing how much she had heard, or what she had heard, about his shoot-out with Cleve Tanner.

"A notch? I hadn't thought anything about it."

All her bitter contempt of the lonely-riding men of violence came into her voice. "Isn't that what the gunmen and the cow thieves always do?"

He was motionless for a long time. Then he drew the skinning knife that always swung at the back of his belt in a worn sheath. Its blade was lean and hollowed, worn almost out of existence by a thousand honings. He stood looking at the knife, then tossed it in the air, and caught it by the handle again.

"I wouldn't go cutting marks on the handle of a gun," he said at last. His voice was thick.

"Nobody cares what anybody does to the handle of a gun."

Roper stepped forward and, with the keen blade, cut a notch clean and deep in the left arm of Dusty's cross.

When he looked at Jody, she was staring at him strangely, almost as if she were afraid.

CHAPTER SIXTEEN

All through the afternoon, Jody Gordon had ridden the barren trails above Ogallala, on a pony that forever tried to turn home. Thaw was on the prairie again, and the South Platte was brimming with melted snow. In the air was something of the damp, clean smell which had marked another spring, in this same place. But it was now more than six months since Jody had seen Bill Roper, and she found it no help that she was forever hearing his name.

Ogallala had grown. The loading chutes along the railroad had more than doubled in two years, and the town itself sprawled farther over the prairie. But the tall white house still stood alone, its foolish wooden towers commanding the long flat reach of the stock corrals.

Wherever Jody rode, she could still see that tallest of the three lookout towers on her father's house—the tower in which she and Bill Roper had sat together through another spring twilight, on a day that now seemed long ago. Nothing could ever remedy the unspeakable emptiness of that house to which Roper would probably never come again, so it was with reluctance that she at last rode up the rise upon which it stood, unlighted, in the dusk.

She unsaddled her own pony, booted it into

the muddy corral, and threw the forty-pound kak onto the saddle-pole with the easy, one-handed swing of the western rider. As she turned toward the house, she was trying not to cry.

Then, as she walked through the stable, a figure rose up from the shadows beside the door and barred her way.

Jody Gordon's breath caught in her throat. She said evenly, "Looking for someone, Bud?"

The spare-framed visitor took off his hat and held it uneasily in his two hands. "Well, I tell you, Miss Gordon—could I speak to you for just a minute?"

"All right. Come on up to the house."

"Well, now, you see—" He kept peering into his hat, flustered by the steady quiet of Jody's fine eyes. "To tell you the truth, Miss Gordon, I'd rather just speak to you here, if it's all the same to you."

Jody said sharply, "There's nobody there but the Chinese cook, and his Mexican wife."

"Well, I'll tell you, Miss Gordon—I'd just as soon leave not be seen around too much, if I can dodge out of it. There's a couple of little misunderstandings has come up between me and your father a couple of times. And, anyway—well, I'll tell you the fact of the matter. I'm a Bill Roper man."

Jody Gordon's heart jumped like a struck pony. "Billy sent you to me?"

"Well, no, I haven't seen Bill Roper for quite some time."

"Oh."

"I'm Shoshone Wilce," the man said. "I rode with Bill Roper in Texas."

There was a little pause, then, in the shadowy dusk of the stable.

Jody said suddenly, "Are you trying to tell me that Billy—that something has happened to Bill Roper?"

"This thing is about your father," Shoshone said.

"If Billy Roper wants anything from my father—"

"I haven't seen Bill Roper. But—I've seen Ben Thorpe. Miss Gordon, tell me one thing: Is your father backing Bill Roper? I mean, is he backing this plowing into Ben Thorpe?"

"My father," Jody Gordon said, "has quit Bill Roper in every way he possibly could. Not one penny of my father's, nor any help of any kind, is back of Bill Roper."

"That's what I thought," Shoshone Wilce said. "Only trouble is, people that don't know the difference, they don't none of them believe that anymore."

"You mean, they think—"

"I get around," Shoshone Wilce reiterated. "I drink with a lot of different people, and they talk. I've drunk with Ben Thorpe himself in Dodge. I've drunk with—"

Jody Gordon interrupted him sharply. "What's happened? You didn't come here to tell me the history of hard liquor in the West!"

"Miss Gordon, your father is in a terrible bad fix. I'm afeard—I'm afeard he's going to die before this thing is through."

"What do you mean?"

"Most people think Lew Gordon is backing Bill Roper—maybe you know that? Well, now there's a feller rode to Ben Thorpe from Miles City—a feller that was a foreman with Thorpe's Montana outfits under Walk Lasham. Maybe this feller had some kind of fight with Lasham—I don't know nothin' about that. But this feller swears to Thorpe that Lasham is letting the Montana herds drain away to the Indians, and to the construction camps, and Ben Thorpe never seeing a penny of the money from beef or hide."

"How do you know this?"

"I was there when this feller come to Ben Thorpe. I stood as close to them as I stand to you when this feller tells Thorpe that Walk Lasham is double-crossing him, and that everything he has in Montana is being gutted out. Thorpe rares up fit to overset the bar. 'You lie!' he says, and this boy says, 'Go count your herds!' And he laughs in Thorpe's face!"

For a moment or two, Shoshone Wilce stared empty-eyed into the dusk, as if he were seeing appalling things.

"But is that true?" Jody demanded.

"Which?"

"Is Bill Roper gutting the Thorpe outfits in Montana?"

"Don't know, myself. But they say he's raising blue hell. They say he's swarming all over Montana, with a bunch of kid renegades behind him, riding like crazy men, and raiding night after night. Some say nobody knows how hard Lasham is hurt, Lasham least of any. And some say Lasham has sold out to Bill Roper, or your father—or both."

"What does Thorpe himself think?"

"Thorpe thinks your father has bought Walk Lasham. Just the same as he thought your father bought Cleve Tanner in Texas, until Bill Roper gunned Cleve down. And Thorpe is fit to be tied. If he loses out in Montana, on top of losing out in Texas, God knows where he'll turn. A man like him—he's terrible dangerous always, Miss Gordon, but now he's ten times more dangerous than he ever was in his life."

"You mean you think Ben Thorpe will—will—"

"Miss Gordon, I know. Ben Thorpe is going to kill Lew Gordon, just as sure as—"

"He wouldn't dare! My father is—is—"

"He'd dare anything. The Texas Rustlers' War put such a sting on his hide as no man can stand—him, least of all! Nobody ever seen nothin' like

Roper's Texas raids—maybe nobody ever will again. You'll see plenty things in the West that couldn't've happened before that! Nobody ever had such a hate as Thorpe has for Roper—he'd kill anybody to get at him. He'd grab you, even, and use you for bait!"

Jody Gordon's eyes had darkened in the dusk, making her face seem very pale. She knew something about the ways of the hard-riding, self-sufficient men of the saddle. The swift action of the guns was as much a part of the background of her life as the fluctuations of the beef market, or the drought which killed the herds.

When she spoke, her voice could hardly be heard. "When is this thing supposed to happen?"

"I don't know. I don't even know where Ben Thorpe is. It might happen tonight, or tomorrow, or next week. But child, it's going to be soon!"

There was a silence, while the eternal bawling of the cattle in the loading pens came to them across the flats.

"What do you want me to do?"

Shoshone Wilce shrugged. "That ain't hardly up to me, Miss Gordon. But I'll tell you this: many's the time I've seen your father go stomping down the boardwalk right here in Ogallala, alone, and not even armed. That won't do, Miss Gordon. If I was in your place, I wouldn't never let him out of the house without his gunbelt strapped on, and the iron free in its leather. And wherever he goes, there ought to be three or four good hard-shooting cowboys with him, because, if I know Ben Thorpe, he isn't going into any gunfight alone!"

"It isn't so easy to boss my father," Jody said. "Even when he's here in Ogallala, which he's not, I often can't change what he does in any way."

Shoshone Wilce moved restlessly in the thickening dark. "Well, I figured I'd better—"

Jody peered at him intently. "What made you bring this word to me?"

"I'm a Bill Roper man," Shoshone Wilce said. "God knows, Miss Gordon, stringing with Bill Roper has never done anything for me. But—well, I just thought Bill Roper would want you to know. I kind of got the idea he thinks a heap of you, Miss Gordon."

Jody Gordon's gloved hands reached out to touch this stranger. She said intensely, "You think he does?"

"Why—didn't aim to speak out of turn. Didn't realize there was ever any doubt."

Jody dropped her hands. "Plenty," she said in a dead voice.

And now another pony came slashing up to the corral, and they heard the wooden ring of the gate bars as the rider kicked them down. One of the loading foremen had come in to file his waybills.

"I got to be getting along," Shoshone Wilce said quickly. "I don't know if you understand, but

I wouldn't want Lew Gordon to hear anything that—"

"I understand," Jody said.

She turned away, but instantly turned back again, and gripped Shoshone's arm just as he was sliding out of sight.

"Stay around," she ordered him. "Stay here until—"

"Miss Gordon," came the quick whisper, "I've got to get on to Miles City. I—"

"I thought so. Bill Roper's somewhere up there, isn't he? Yes. Well, I'm going to join my father there—I'll ride with you in the morning."

"Four hundred miles! And no coach until—"

"Don't worry about that. It takes saddle ponies to make time."

"But—I'm afraid your Paw might think—"

"I don't know how Bill Roper ever used you," Jody said with contempt.

Shoshone winced. "I—I'll be around."

He faded into the shadows as Jody walked out of the stable, her eyes hard and bright in the dusk.

CHAPTER SEVENTEEN

Bill Roper sat alone at a rear table in the Palace Bar, in Miles City—the young, turbulent center of a vast, raw range, the possibilities of which were still unknown. A swamper was going about the great square room, lighting the swinging oil lamps, and the foot rail along the bar was beginning to fill. Roper pulled his slouch hat over one eye and watched the goings and comings of the rope-and-saddle men. The Palace Bar had faro, roulette, and girls. Roper could rest assured that every cowboy in Miles City would at least look in here in the course of the evening.

For three months, Roper had ridden through the bitter Montana winter. It had been no trouble for him to sweep together a dozen malcontent cowboys who hated Lasham, or Thorpe, or both. Already, they knew Bill Roper's name. Against their common enemy, these youngsters could be led, wild, reckless, and crazy for raid, and Roper had led them as Texas had taught him.

His new northern wild bunch faced conditions in many ways bitterly adverse. Here in the north were no ousted cattlemen, no established population to which he could look for help. The Canadian border was far away, and no market awaited the hard-pushed herds on the other side.

What Montana had that Texas did not have was a concentration of Indian tribes, principally Sioux and Cheyenne, deprived of their hunting grounds, and dependent for food upon beef which the government was pledged to supply. It was to this circumstance that Roper had turned.

The giant beef contracts that the government threw upon the market had inevitably attracted more than one kind of graft. Indian agents sent from the east, without experience in either Indians or cattle, made easy dupes for unscrupulous cattlemen of Walk Lasham's stamp. Others less readily cheated but, willing to retire rich, had cooperated with Lasham in sidetracking beef which the government paid for but which no Indian ever saw. The result was famine—pitiful, relentless. Starvation stalked through the lodges of the Sioux, the Cheyenne, the Crow—and with it, Roper's opportunity.

Scouring the country, Roper turned up four Indian agents who were already badly scared. They had overplayed their hands and were now faced with a loss of life among their charges, about which they could do nothing without revealing their own corrupt inefficiency. These men had connived with Lasham in bringing about a condition of tribal starvation; they were willing to connive with Bill Roper to cover up their position in any way they could.

By delivering beef to the reservations under

these highly irregular conditions, Roper's wild bunch could do little more than make expenses. But the advantage was this—a beef herd delivered to an Indian tribe disappeared overnight, leaving little trace. A thousand hands skinned out the beef, destroying the portions of the hides containing the brands.

Constantly changing horses, perpetually in the saddle, Roper's saddle hawks swung across Montana. They first struck at Muddy Bend, picking up four hundred head of steers in the breaks of the Yellowstone. Three days' hard driving delivered these to a village of Assiniboine. Only four days later, they were on the flats of the Little Thunder, far away. Here, struggling through a soft, blinding snow, they ran off five hundred head, and a few days later, three hundred more. They Christmased in company with a herd of lifted steers somewhere between Three Sleep and the Little Powder, and New Year's found them sifting the pick of Lasham's cattle out of his Lost Soldier range.

By the end of January, they had moved three thousand head—the very cream of the wintering stock. Repeatedly, they had driven cattle incredible distances in impossible time, they had gathered fat steers under the very noses of Lasham's winter riders, and their raids had covered an area of country which reasonable men would not even have attempted to travel. Roper, looking back over the winter as he now sat in the Palace Bar, knew he had done the best he could.

Yet he knew his work had only begun. All their hard riding would fail of effect unless he could strike such a smashing blow as would cause a split between Lasham and Ben Thorpe.

In a vast country that seemed to crawl with Lasham's herds, serious inroads seemed impossible, but now, for once, the times had fitted themselves to Roper's purpose. The beef market was unsteadying at the very time it should have strengthened, and the Rocky Mountain silver booms were draining away the capital upon which the cowmen had relied. Rumors of disaster were running all over the West. No man could tell now what the spring would bring. Any appreciable damage to Walk Lasham might turn the tide against him, leading to his smash-up with the melt-off of the snows.

And Roper had a plan—rash in scope and method, but savage in effect if it could be fulfilled. Already, he had enough riders in sight to strike this last desperate blow. But the men available to his purpose were wild-eyed fighting kids who could not be driven and could scarcely be led, and Roper could not captain his campaign alone. So now he fretted in Miles City, seeking three or four outlaw leaders who would make his preparations complete.

He could not stay here long. The heavy rewards

Thorpe had upon his head were less dangerous to him than the inevitable appearance of Lasham himself, who was sure to be well supported by good gunfighting riders, too many for any one man to face.

Still studying everyone who came into the bar, Roper broke open a deck of cards and laid out a hand of solitaire.

Now, one of the dance hall girls came to his table, slipping uninvited into a chair. This was a girl whose attention bothered and embarrassed Roper every time he came here. She no longer hung upon him as she had at first, but it seemed that when Roper was in the room, she could think of nothing else. Her name was Marquita.

He didn't know what attracted her to him; he didn't know what attracted any particular woman to any particular man. Undoubtedly, she had discovered who he was, and perhaps the stories about him that had come up the Trail from Texas—stories already exaggerated to the magnitude of whoppers—partly explained her notice. Or perhaps she would have noticed him if she had not found out his name at all. To the Palace Bar came all manner of the lean-carved saddle men of the Trail—hard-drinking, swaggering men extremely interested in the dance hall girls. But Roper, who drank steadily, alone, without ever becoming drunk, never swaggered at all, and his eyes, which quietly missed nothing, habitually passed over this girl without interest. It may be that his very disinterest was what caught her attention first and later gave him the desirability of the unobtainable.

She spoke to him now in a quiet, lifeless voice. "Why don't you like me?"

He swung his head to look at her, as expressionless as a horse. He neither liked nor disliked her. He had known a good many girls of her particular status at both ends of the Long Trail. Some of them he knew to have left homes in which they should have been glad to stay. It was his belief that some wild gypsy strain in these girls prompted them to choose the tumultuous adventures of the unknown, rather than the hard, drab lives that fell to the lot of cowmen's wives. Certainly, any one of them could have married off, in the beginning. If they found out later that what they had chosen was arduous and tawdry, by that time it was too late.

"I like you all right," he said.

"No, you don't. You don't even see me at all."

He noticed now that she looked different tonight, and after a moment, he recognized that this was because there was no paint on her face. That would be because he disliked paint—though he had no idea how she had found that out. Her washed face was a perfectly symmetrical oval set with black eyes a little slanted, and her black hair, parted in the middle, was drawn back severely, in the fashion of the mestizo girls of the Texas border.

She leaned toward him now and spoke rapidly, her voice low and compelling. “Listen—I hate Walk Lasham, too.”

One of Bill Roper’s eyebrows flickered. His first thought was that Lasham himself had hired this girl to spy upon him.

“Why?”

“Because you do,” Marquita said.

“You know who I am, then,” he suggested.

“Yes, I found that out.” Her face was child-like and tired, but behind its resignation a certain intensity burned.

Roper dropped his eyes to his game, but Marquita’s slim hand shot out to grip one of his.

“Listen,” she insisted. “You have to listen to me. Walk Lasham’s in town. He came in this afternoon.”

So, Roper thought, the time had come to move on again, with his work undone. He didn’t like it much.

“Well, thanks,” he said, “I’m glad to know.”

“He knows you’re here—and what you’re here for.”

“I suppose he does,” Roper said.

“You’re waiting here for Lasham,” she accused him. “You know he’ll come here. You’re going to try shooting it out—”

Roper shrugged and was silent.

"Bill, it's hopeless! Walk Lasham is the fastest gunfighter in the north!"

Roper shrugged again. "Walk wants no fight with me."

"You're going to force the fight yourself! That's what you've been waiting here for, ever since you came to Miles City. Any moment Lasham may walk in that door—"

"Well?"

"You think I want to see you killed?"

He turned to his cards, impatiently. "I wouldn't worry about it if I were you."

"Can't anything ever turn you at all?"

"No."

Marquita sat staring at him hopelessly, in her eyes a fixity of devotion which his taciturnity seemed to increase. Against his will he was becoming aware that something was happening to Marquita. There was enough untouched fire in that girl to burn a long time. Perhaps it was already too late to end their curiously one-sided relationship here, or prevent its cropping up at other times, other places, with results that could not be foreseen.

He remained silent, and in a little while, she went away.

An hour passed, while Roper, drinking slowly, played his solitaire and watched the door.

Then suddenly, Marquita was back. She came behind his chair to speak close to his ear in a panicky whisper. “He’s coming! He’s coming along the walk—”

“All right.”

“Walk has two of his men with him,” she said rapidly. “You haven’t a chance, not a ghost of a chance. I can’t bear to see you killed! I know you don’t care anything about me. If you did, I’d go anywhere in the world with you. But now you have to come out of here—quick—by the back way. I’ll do anything—”

Roper turned his head to look up into her face, very close to his. There was more to this girl than there was to the rest of her kind. Even now, he was unable to recognize that Marquita was capable of a sincerity of purpose and a passionate preoccupation in her purpose, not to be expected here. “I wouldn’t step aside two feet,” he told her, “to pass Walk or any man. I tell you, Walk won’t fight!”

“It’s you I’m afraid of! You’re the hardest—”

Suddenly, she whimpered. Bill Roper saw that three men had come into the front of the Palace Bar.

The first of the three, a dark, lean man with wide, bowed shoulders, was Walk Lasham.

Marquita caught Bill’s head in her arms, forced up his chin, and kissed him. He was surprised at the unexpected softness of her lips, hot against his mouth. Then abruptly Marquita stooped, and as she sprang away from him, he felt the weight of his gunbelt ease. She flung over her shoulder, "It's for your own sake!" Her face was white, frightened.

He half started up, in instant anger, but the girl was running down the room. He saw her put something under the bar, and he knew it was his gun.

Roper banged his whiskey glass upon the table, trying to catch a bartender's eye. If Lasham had not seen what the girl had done, one of them could bring him his gun before it was too late. But the bar was thronged, the bartenders working fast in the thick of the evening rush.

The barflies had made room for Walk Lasham at the end of the bar, and Lasham and his two cowboys had their heads together now, consulting.

One of the cowboys, a man with a scar across his face that distorted his mouth in the manner of a hare lip, went quickly behind the bar, hunted beneath it, and returned to Walk. Roper saw Lasham's long face set. He said to himself, "Walk knows . . ."

Walk Lasham was fiddling with his empty glass on the bar, and the scar-mouthed man was watching Roper covertly with one eye from under the brim of his hat. Lasham reached for a bottle, filled his glass, and tossed it off. Then he turned squarely toward Roper and came walking back through the big room.

Roper played his cards, his hands visible upon the table. It seemed to take Lasham a long time to walk the length of the room. Roper glanced at the lookout chair, where a salaried gun-fighter usually sat. It was empty now.

Walk Lasham was standing in front of him.

"So you," he said, "are the tough gunman that killed Cleve Tanner."

Bill Roper raised his eyes to Walk Lasham's face. "And you," he said, "are one of the dirty cowards that murdered Dusty King."

Sparks jumped in Lasham's eyes and instantly disappeared again.

"And I suppose," Walk Lasham said, "it's in your mind to get me, one of these times?"

"When I'm ready, I'll get you, all right."

Lasham drew a deep breath and held it for a moment; the corners of his nostrils were white. "Well—I'm here."

A hush had fallen upon the room, unbroken by the clink of a glass or the rattle of a chip. Lasham and Roper looked at each other through a moment of silence, while the bartenders stood immobile among their bottles, and men who feared they were in the line of fire moved out of the way, stepping softly.

"Not ready, now?" Lasham said.

"You'll know it when I am."

"*I* happen to be ready now!"

He dropped his eyes to Roper's hands, and his

own right hand started a tentative movement toward the butt of his gun. His spread fingers shook a little as his hand crept down. But he was grinning now, sure of his ground.

"Looks a little different to you now, huh?"

"A coyote always looks like a coyote to me."

The smile dropped from Lasham's face. "I'm going to give you every chance," he said. His voice swung in even rhythms, low and sing-song. "I'm going to count to five. Draw and fire any time you want to, because on five, I'm going to kill you where you sit."

"I don't think you are."

"One, two—" Lasham said.

Roper scratched his left shoulder with his right hand. He was trying to reach the back of his chair with his fingertips, for he believed now that that was his only hope—to buck the gun with the chair.

"Three!"

But now the scar-mouthed man spoke suddenly. From his position at one side, he had dared flick his eyes to the door. "Walk, look out! Don't turn! Watch this buzzard, but wheel back and stand by me!"

Into the front of the bar, two men had come. They came striding back the length of the room, their spurs ringing brokenly. Roper did not see their guns come out. But suddenly, the weapons of both of them appeared in their hands, smoothly and easily, from no place.

The two men were Lee Harnish and Tex Long.

Tex Long's .45 clicked in the palm of his hand as it came to full cock. He said, "Howdy, Bill. A girl just brought us word. Dave Shannon and Hat Crick Tommy are up the street. And Dry Camp Pierce."

"Jesus," Lee Harnish said, "we've been hunting you for two months! You want us to blast these Indians, boss?"

Bill Roper drew a deep breath and grinned. At first, he could not even appreciate that here, at last, were the leaders he needed for his great raid. All he could think of was that he had been reprieved from certain death, and he knew that life was good.

CHAPTER EIGHTEEN

The tribute implied by the re-gathering of the wild bunch leaders was one of the most extraordinary things that had ever happened in Bill Roper's life. There was not much to their story. Driven out of Texas on the eve of Bill Roper's victory, for a while, they had gone their separate ways. But gradually they had drifted together again, in the Indian nations, at Dodge, in the northern cow camps. With Cleve Tanner broken in Texas and the roots cut from under Ben Thorpe's organization by the loss of his breeding grounds, the outlaw riders found themselves unwilling to leave their work unfinished. So at last they had come looking for Roper—and had found him.

None of them had much to say. "A couple of us ain't doing anything right now," Lee Harnish said casually. "We figured maybe you could get us some sewing to do."

With these men, Roper had busted the toughest organization in Texas. There was a bare chance that with them he could accomplish the impossible again, this time in the north.

"Yeah," he said, keeping to himself the stir of warlike triumph their arrival had brought him. "Might be I could help you out! Can any of you boys ride a horse?"

The first thing was to get them out of there. The open gathering in Miles City of the same outlawed riders who had smashed Cleve Tanner in Texas was a gauge of battle that Walk Lasham would be forced to take up. Roper was not ready for that and might not be ready for many weeks.

He therefore named as rendezvous a lonely shanty on Fork Creek and hazed his reunited wild bunch out of town by ones and twos, before Walk Lasham could get into action.

Roper himself was the last to ride out of Miles City. Seasoned night riders though these men might be, with names now famous the length of the trail, most of them were youngsters still. Not one of them could be trusted not to get a skinful of liquor and go gunning for Lasham's men on his own hook.

Roper was relieved, therefore, upon riding into the Fork Creek rendezvous in the dreary February twilight, to find his Texas men already waiting for him there. They were eating fresh beef, but not their own, as Roper came into the little cabin, stamping the snow off his boots.

"Glad to see you're eating again," Roper said. "We've got to up-stakes, mighty soon."

Lee Harnish looked sheepish. "Say, I forgot something. I got a letter for you here."

Roper took the worn envelope and stood turning it over in his hands. The date showed it to be three weeks old—no great age, everything considered. But what took hold of him, so that for a full minute he dared not break the seal, was that the letter was from Jody Gordon.

"Where—where'd you get this?"

"I got it off the Wells Fargo man at Sundance. You'd already come on here when I was there."

Roper ripped open the envelope. The weather-faced riders in the little cabin ostentatiously avoided watching his face as he read. The whole note covered no more than half a page, but as he folded it and put it into a pocket, his hands were shaking in a way that would have cost him his life if he had been walking into a gunfight then. There was a long silence.

"What you got figured, Bill?" Hat Crick Tommy was asking.

With a visible effort, Roper pulled himself together. Briefly, he told them what his new wild bunch had done.

"But we haven't even scratched the surface," he finished. "Unless we hit Walk Lasham quick and hard, Thorpe will get his balance again, and reach his roots back into Texas, and all the work we did down there will be for nothing."

"Me," Tex Long said, "I aim to swing with you, and try to finish up what we begun. But, way I see it, the layout up here is terrible bad, for our style of work."

Dry Camp Pierce spoke for the first time.

"Worst thing is, we've got no place to get rid of our stock, even if we lift it. If all those boys we had with us in Texas was here, we could run some bunches southeast to the railroad camps and maybe try some drives down into Wyoming. But the way we're fixed—"

"There isn't any profit in the way I figured," Roper admitted. "I've been taking a pasear up along the Canadian border. I figure it's an easy drive. If you criminals are willing to come on and take one more crack at Thorpe and Lasham—"

"There's no one beyond the border that's needing any stock," Dry Camp Pierce said gloomily.

"Dry Camp," Bill Roper said, "I'm thinking of the tribes."

There was a moment's silence. "Granting that Canada's full of war paint," Tex Long said, "how the devil—"

"I've talked to Iron Dog."

Every one of them, each in his own way, pricked up his ears at that. Iron Dog was a famous warrior chief of the Gros Ventre Sioux. Ragged and starving, his decimated band driven far out of their home country, Iron Dog was no longer the stubbornly resisting force that had once made his name. But though he was broken and helpless now, remnants of his leadership remained; his influence extended over many bands, and more than one tribe.

"I don't hold with dealing with red men much," Dave Shannon said.

"These bucks are forced out of their ranges without any deal made whereby they get fed," Roper said. "Half of them are in as pitiful a state of starvation as you ever saw. A big part of the blame for that is on Walk Lasham. Now I aim to square the deal."

"Starvation, some say, is good for Indians," Dry Camp said. "Makes 'em more pious."

"I already made us a rendezvous with Iron Dog, before I knew you were in on this," Bill Roper told them now. "Inside of a month, Iron Dog will be camped on the Milk River with seven or eight bands."

"Seven or eight bands!" Tex Long shouted at him. "My God, there'll be worse than a thousand Indians on the Milk!"

"A thousand, hell!" Roper said. "If there aren't that many buck warriors alone, I'll eat the beef myself!"

The men in this little cabin were not easily surprised, and less easily shocked or awed, but their usually unrevealing faces now gave them away.

"God Almighty!" Dave Shannon said. It was almost a prayer.

"He's done it now," Hat Crick Tommy said slowly. "You know what happens when you throw that many loose Indians together? You got a war on your hands, by God! They'll come whooping down Montana—they'll tear the country wide open! The whole frontier will go up in a bust of smoke. Nothing'll ever stop 'em, once they get together like that!"

"One thing will."

"What will?"

"Grub," said Roper.

"That might be so," Dave Shannon admitted. "I never yet see an Indian go to war on a full stomach . . ."

A tension had come into that dark cabin. They were realizing now that they stood in the shadow of events of a magnitude they had not dreamed. In the quiet, Bill Roper's hands kept creasing and re-creasing the letter from Jody Gordon. A faint dampness showed on his forehead, but his fingers felt cold and awkward.

"There's five of us here," Tex Long said. "You expect us to just suddenly feed every Indian in creation?"

"I've got twenty-seven riders waiting to throw in with us at the first word."

"Twenty-seven riders? Where?"

"All over Montana. What do you think I did all winter? Holed up like a she-bear, and had cubs?"

Silence again, while they all studied Roper.

"How many you figure to move?" Tex Long asked at last.

Roper's voice was so low they could hardly

hear his words. "Between twenty and thirty thousand head."

Tex Long threw his hat against the roof poles in a gesture of complete impatience. "Dead of winter," he said, "maybe having to fight part of the time . . . Why, thirty-forty cowboys couldn't drive—"

"We don't have to handle this stock like fat beef," Roper reminded him. "We don't have to pull up for quicksand, or stampede losses, or high water. If a hundred head get swept down a river, what the hell? Some different Indians will get hold of 'em downstream. Working that way, hard and fast, thirty cowboys can move every head in Montana!"

"We're terrible short of time," Tex Long said.

"I know it. In another couple of months, their chuck wagons will be heading out, and the deep grass will be full of their riders. We have to move and move quick."

"What do they look like, these twenty-seven riders you got?"

"Mainly cowhands—laid off for the winter. Every one of 'em hates Lasham's guts; none of 'em look for any pay."

"It might be," Dry Camp Pierce declared himself, "it just could be done." A hard gleam was coming into the old rustler's wary eyes. "And if it can—great God! There's never been nothing like this!"

The others seemed to have had the breath knocked out of them by the unheard-of scope, the bold daring, the headlong all-or-nothing character of the plan.

"This is bigger than the Texas raids," Tex Long said wonderingly. "This is bigger than anything has ever been!"

Suddenly, Dave Shannon smacked his thigh with his huge hand. "By God, I believe it'll bust 'em!"

Over the pack of outlawed youngsters had come a wave of that fanatic enthusiasm which sometimes sways men as they face the impossible, but Roper, strangely, was unable to share it. The great raid he had planned all winter now seemed futile—a plan senseless and cold.

"Bill," said Lee Harnish, "what's the matter with you? You got chills and fever, or something?"

Roper spoke to Harnish alone, as if he had forgotten the others. "That letter was from Jody Gordon," he said.

"Bad news, son?"

"I don't know. She wants me to come to Ogallala."

"When?"

"Now—right away."

"What for? Does she say?"

"She says she needs me . . . she says she needs me bad, and right away. I guess she does, all right. If she didn't, I don't believe she'd ever write to me."

There was silence in the little cabin.

"Bill," said Lee Harnish at last, "if you quit on us now—" He stopped.

Dry Camp said, "You reckon something's happened to Lew Gordon?"

"Looks like she'd say, if that was it."

"Hell musta bust some place," Pierce said. "I know that girl; those people don't holler before they're hit."

Roper lifted his eyes from the floor to look at the others. He had never dared to hope he would hear from Jody Gordon, of her own initiative. The piece of paper upon which she had written, the handwriting that was her own, seemed to bring her suddenly near and close, nearer than the cabin walls, nearer than his side-riders here in the room. She always had the ability to get inside his defenses and break his heart with a glance or a word.

The faces of the wild bunch riders were expressionless, noncommittal. Roper knew they wouldn't have much to say. They were youngsters still—all except Pierce. But their faces were carved lean and hard by long riding, and a lot of that riding had been for him.

He stood up, shaking his shoulders.

"Catch up your ponies."

"We pulling out? Tonight yet?"

"You bet your life we are. Ought to make Red Horse Springs by midnight."

"And after that," Harnish said slowly, "what is it, Bill? Is it Ogallala?"

Once more, the silence while they waited for Bill.

"It's the raid," Roper said.

CHAPTER NINETEEN

Lew Gordon came stumping across the corral of his little Miles City house, his spurs ringing at every stride. His big hands, rope-hardened and thickened at the knuckles, swung loose at his sides, but his face had the look of a man beset.

Here was a man born and bred to the rigors of the saddle, and competent to face them, even yet, but now he was face to face with necessities other than those of the plainsmen. At this hour in his life, Lew Gordon controlled a greater potential wealth and power than that of most international bankers. The obscure, inadequate figures in his tally books had multiplied in meaning, even since the death of Dusty King. He found himself now fighting a desperate battle of his own, in which no man was equipped to help him. And like all truly great battles, it was one which a blind courage, however stubborn, could not win.

No pomp and circumstance marked the life of Lew Gordon, master of an empire though he might be. Like his daughter, he usually unsaddled his own horse as he came in, and with his calloused hands rubbed away the bridle itch from his pony's jaw and poll before he kicked it loose. Only, his eyes had a far-off look now, and his hands dangled lank as he walked, unready for the gun which they had forgotten to belt about his still-lean hips.

Opening the back door of the house, he sent a great roar through the walls—"Jody! Jody, where are you?"

She answered him, and Lew Gordon, picking up a cold steak from a platter always left for him in the kitchen, went to find her, tearing off mouthfuls of beef as he walked.

"What's the meaning of this?" was his greeting as his daughter came running to him through the house. "You were supposed to stay in Ogallala!"

Jody threw her arms about his neck and pulled his head down to kiss him, but Lew Gordon was not to be put off.

"That horse wrangler just brought me word that you was here," he said. "There's a pretty kettle of soap, when some horse wrangler knows more about where a man's daughter is at than he knows himself! How in heck did you get here?"

"I rode, Dad. I couldn't send you word I was coming because I came faster than the mail could come through."

"You rode? Alone? Better'n four hundred miles across all that—say!"

"Some cowboys were riding up this way," she told him.

"Cowboys! What's the good of that? I won't stand for it! You ain't a child anymore. This thing of larruping all over the country with a pack of saddle tramps—damn my soul if I ever heard the beat!"

"Dad—I want to talk to you."

"Darned if I know how I'm ever going to get you raised. You don't pay any more attention to what I say than as if—"

"Dad, will you please sit down? I tell you, I want to talk to you!"

"Oh, all right." Lew Gordon flopped into a chair, jabbed his spurs into the floor at long range, and tore off another huge mouthful of beef.

"There are two pieces of bad news," Jody said now. "First thing, Ben Thorpe has cut under us in the bidding for the government contracts at Dodge."

A spark leaped into Lew Gordon's eyes. Under the pressure of the last two years, he had turned edgy and garrulous, as if his mind had become hasty on the trigger, now that his hands were idle. "I might have known it!" his big voice boomed. "Those infernal—"

Nowadays, a vast swarm of intricacies, having to do with markets, costs, and the holding of land, made a puzzle through which Lew Gordon could hardly find his way. The raw materials with which he traded were those he understood—cattle and grass lands, horses, guns, and men. But the rise of the West had now brought the old cowman to the necessities of a financier and a politician—

even to those of a statesman. What the bankers with their precise figures could never understand was that Lew Gordon's problems involved the conflicting wills of a thousand men.

Under the prophetic leadership of Dusty King, King-Gordon had become great. Few empires had ever included more latent power than lay in the miles of loading chutes, the thousands of head of horses, the countless cattle now literally scattered from border to border under the many King-Gordon brands. Small wonder that the old cowman's rope-gnarled hands sometimes moved uncertainly, now that he, alone, was King-Gordon . . .

"The loss of those contracts is going to hurt," Jody said. "I've brought the books up into fair shape, and it looks to me as if King-Gordon is starting the worst year in history. If the losses go on piling up the way they are—"

"Everybody is up against losses," Lew Gordon growled. "I guess we can stand it if anybody can. What's the other bad news?"

Jody Gordon came and sat on the arm of her father's chair. "There was a man who rode up to Ogallala from Dodge City," she said. "He brought some very peculiar news, and I don't like it at all."

"If that renegade Colorado outfit thinks they're going to—" Lew Gordon began.

"This was a Bill Roper man," Jody said.

Lew Gordon checked as suddenly as if he had been struck across the face. His voice stopped, and he stopped chewing his beef, and for a few moments, every fiber in his body seemed to relax . . . except that his eyes remained alive, fixed upon the eyes of his daughter, and the new light that came into them was a light that burned.

When Lew Gordon spoke, his voice was so quiet that its very stillness carried the threat of imminent destruction. "Bill Roper sent a man to you?"

"I didn't say that. He's a man who was with Bill Roper in the Texas Rustlers' War; he doesn't seem to be in the Montana raids. In the Texas war, he rode for Bill Roper as a scout, I think. I guess you'll admit that the men who scouted for Roper in Texas knew their business."

"Who was it?" Lew Gordon rumbled. "What's his name?"

"Shoshone Wilce."

"Wilce! I know that name. I know it well. I'd rope and drag him in a second, if I caught him talking to you!"

"This man has talked with Ben Thorpe in Dodge," Jody told her father. "A lot of strange news is working down to Thorpe from up here in Montana. Some bands of rustlers are slashing up and down Montana, throwing lead and leather into the Thorpe outfits under Lasham. They say he's badly hurt already—nobody will know how badly until the winter breaks. They say—"

"Well," her father interrupted her, "everybody knows that. If you made this fool trip to tell me that Montana law has gone to hell on a pinto, you've wasted your—"

"That isn't all," Jody insisted. "They say there's going to be a split between Thorpe and Lasham. They say that nobody knows who is behind the rustling that is cutting into the Thorpe herds under Lasham, but Thorpe thinks—"

"Nobody knows?" Gordon repeated with impatience. "Everybody knows! Don't you know?"

Jody hesitated. "Yes," she admitted, "I suppose I do."

"This is Bill Roper's work," Lew Gordon said. "It's getting so a man can recognize his style a hundred mile off! The same wild bunch that was with him in Texas is with him again, and no rider comes into Miles City without packing in a new rumor about some damn' devilment. Why, just last week, Roper and Tex Long and Lee Harnish were seen strutting up and down openly, in the streets of this town. Dry Camp Pierce is supposed to be tied up with him, and that little gunthrower that calls himself Hat Crick Tommy. Roper has pulled outlawed gunfighters up into Montana until it ain't safe for a decent citizen to ride the range!"

"Have we lost any stock? Has anybody, except Walk Lasham?"

"What's that got to do with it? Law that's worthless to one outfit is worthless to everybody else. All my life, I've fought for law and order more than any other one thing. I've wanted to see the cow country made into a decent place to live at. And now this renegade kid, that was practically raised under my own roof—he's working a damage to the range that will set us back twenty years before he's through!"

Jody Gordon was silent for a minute. "It's Ben Thorpe that I want to talk to you about," she said at last.

Her father waited, his eyes angry.

"The word from Dodge explains half the trouble that King-Gordon is up against," Jody said. "Thorpe can't believe that one lone cowboy, deserted by everyone who should have been his friend, could manage to smash his Texas holdings and go on to cut away his herds in Montana. He thought that we were backing Billy Roper in the Texas Rustlers' War. And he believes that we're backing him now. He thinks that King-Gordon is behind the Montana raids, and he holds you responsible for everything that Roper has done. That's why he's fighting King-Gordon so desperately, in the markets, in the government bidding, wherever we turn—"

"Well?" Lew Gordon said. "You mean to say you came all this way to tell me that?"

"But that isn't all!"

"Well?" Gordon said again.

"Ben Thorpe means to kill you."

Lew Gordon's face showed no change of expression. But he did not reply at once.

"I don't doubt it," he said at last, "what would you expect? You bring war into a range, and anybody is likely to go down."

"But what can we do?"

"What is there to do? As long as Bill Roper is on the loose, this is the kind of goings-on we'll have. But mark you, I'm a long way from through. We'll beat—"

Jody's face was white. She said in a level voice, "If Thorpe means to get you, he'll get you all right."

"By God," said Gordon, "nobody's got me yet!"

"That was because you never forgot the tools you were working with. Because you were thinking of horses and men instead of pastures and dollars. Because, until now, you always had Dusty King—"

"I don't see exactly," Lew said, "why you bring Dusty in."

"Because Dusty King is dead. Because he was killed by the same men who want to kill you!"

"You know what's at the bottom of all the trouble we're having," her father said. "You know as well as I do that two years of nothing but trouble lays square at the door of Bill Roper."

Jody sprang up to face him. "I certainly do not know anything of the kind!" she answered him.

Lew Gordon stared at her.

"It's an everlasting shame upon the cow country that Dusty King's killers are still in their saddles. I tell you, Billy Roper is the only man I've seen with courage enough to—"

And now her father angered as she had seldom seen him anger. "You'll tell me nothing!" he roared. "Roper! I'm sick of hearing his name—a dirty outlaw whelp that knows nothing but kill and burn and raid! Better for him, and for us all, if Dusty had let him die on the old Sedalia trail, with his Dad!"

Jody's eyes narrowed and filled with tears. "You may as well know this," she told her father. "The day that Billy Roper dies, I want to die, too."

For a moment, Lew Gordon seemed bewildered. He stared at his daughter as if the devil had come up through the floor. The girl who faced him was entirely strange to him.

He heard her say, "If you had stayed by him, as Dusty King would have done, Thorpe would have been whipped and through, long ago."

"Child," he said queerly, "what are you talking about?"

"If you'd only take Billy Roper back into King-Gordon—"

"That'll never happen while I live," her father said flatly.

A silence fell between them, presently broken by the girl. "He asked me to ride with him once, when he first took the outlaw trail. I wish I had. To the last day I live, I'll wish I'd ridden with him then. And now I'll tell you something more. If ever he asks me again, I'll go."

At first, her father's bewilderment seemed increased. Before now, he had always looked at her as a child, just a baby—even when she had in some part taken over the ledgers which now guided his work. But now he saw that Jody had changed—had become something new and strange to him. Belatedly, Lew Gordon perhaps now perceived that his daughter had not been a child for a long time.

For several moments, he stared at her, more shaken than he had been since the death of Dusty King. Then his face congested, and he rose up on his boot heels to tower over the girl.

"By God," he said, his voice unsteady with the repression he put upon it, "that closes the deal! I've kept my riders off him because of Dusty King, and I let him run on and on, rousing up a range war that has close to busted King-Gordon. But when it comes to tampering with you—it's the end! I'm through, you hear me?"

"Dad!"

"If it's the last thing I'll ever do, I'll clean the range of him—so help me God!"

He caught up his battered sombrero, and his spurs rang as he turned toward the door.

"Dad, what are you going to do?"

"Thorpe has a reward on Bill Roper's head. King-Gordon is going to double that reward."

"But Dad, Dad, can't you see—"

"I see he's an outlaw and a renegade. In Texas, that's the same as a coyote—and we stamp them out of the range!"

He went storming out, his face black and violent with portent of war.

For several moments, Jody Gordon stood motionless where he had left her. Then she turned and went out of the house to the long shed-like stable.

Shoshone Wilce was loitering there in the shadow of the rear wall, an uneasy and restless figure.

"Did you find out where Billy Roper can be reached?" Jody demanded.

"Yes, ma'am, I kind of did, I guess, and I got to be getting on there, Miss Gordon. If you'll just give me any message you want me to take, I'd sure like to be pulling out of here, before—"

"Where is he?"

"Why, seems like he has some kind of a hole-up camp somewheres up Fork Crick. I know about where it would be, I think. I figure I better—"

"All right. You be here with two good horses just after dark."

"If you could just give me the message now, I'd sure like to—"

"There is no message. I'm going with you to Bill Roper."

Shoshone stared at her, unbelieving. "Hey! Wait a minute! I can't—"

"You'll do as I say, Shoshone."

Shoshone Wilce looked like a man entrapped. "I can't do it! Your father—I just won't do it, Miss Gordon!"

"All right. I'll make the ride by myself."

"Hey, look! You can't—"

"Bill Roper isn't going to like this, Wilce."

Shoshone studied her searchingly but found nothing to reassure him. It was in his mind that this girl would do exactly as she said. "My life ain't worth a nickel, either way," he almost whimpered.

"You be here with the horses," Jody said.

She turned and went into the house, leaving Shoshone Wilce standing unhappy and uncertain, ankle deep in the wet snow.

CHAPTER TWENTY

The rounding up of the wild bunch riders lost Roper a few days, but within the week, Bill Roper and Tex Long rode into the plains of the Little Dry. Snow was falling again, and it came down in huge flakes, soft, wet, and heavy, blinding the range. Through this slow smother, the men under Roper and Long pushed steadily, carrying with them more than forty head of loose horses lately obtained from the Rosebud Sioux to camp at last in the lee of a low flat butte.

Here around a spluttering fire, the riders crouched in their sodden blankets, like Indians, while Roper gave out his orders. Their faces, clouded by lack of razoring, showed gaunt and bony in the orange light of the fire, and over their blanketed shoulders the snow fell steadily, as if the prairie were trying in its formless way to blot out the fire and the men.

Thirty-two men and six outlaw leaders were now in the field against Walk Lasham's powerful Montana outfits in the Great Raid. Thirty-eight picked men—most of them gunfighters, all of them crack cowboys—concentrated in a single wild bunch under a chief who knew his ground!

Their force was strong enough to have called itself a company of cavalry—and it would have been a good one. There were enough of them to have captured Miles City or Ogallala, or they could have handled twenty-five thousand head of cattle in a single bunch. They numbered more than twice as many as the party of buffalo hunters who had beaten off the siege of a thousand Indians—the picked warriors of half a dozen tribes—at the battle of Adobe Walls.

Roper's first move had been to split his renegade riders into five bunches under the leaders that he knew—Tex Long, Lee Harnish, Dave Shannon, Dry Camp Pierce, and himself. Hat Crick Tommy he sent to Miles City in search of further word from Jody Gordon; Hat Crick would later rejoin Roper as messenger and scout.

Dry Camp Pierce was in charge, in a general way, of most of the wild bunch; he was to sweep westward across Montana, raiding as he went. By running the cattle northward in relays to Iron Dog's people, Pierce could strike hard, gut a choice range, and two days later launch a new raid a hundred miles away.

It was Roper's plan that he and Tex Long, with twelve men between them, should make the most daring raid of all, a raid upon the big herds which Lasham held between the headwaters of Timber Creek and the Little Dry. Of all the ranges in which the wild bunch was interested, this was the nearest to Miles City—the most accessible, the most closely watched, the best protected. How many cattle he could transfer from this range to the starving Canadian Sioux, Roper did not know, but it was his hope to raise such a conspicuous and stubborn disturbance as would mask the operations of the rest of the wild bunch, and permit Pierce to work unimpeded.

"The fourteen of us will split seven ways," Roper told them now. "I figure Lasham's lookout camp for this range is about twelve miles southeast. We'll comb every way but that way. I'm not telling you how to gather stock. Hunt 'em like you know how to hunt 'em. Move out one day's ride, spotting your cow bunches. Next day, pick 'em up and work 'em this way. And on the third day, throw your gather against a coulee or something, where one man can hold 'em, and the other man of each pair ride back and meet me here. I figure this range is heavy with cattle. "I don't see any reason why two good men can't easy throw together three hundred head in a couple of days. That gives us a nice bunch of about two thousand. The more the better—but with two thousand, we'll make our drive."

"You want we should cut for grade at all?"

"Drive everything—don't stop to cut. If you fall in with some big bunches, more'n you can handle, let the poor stock and the mosshorns go to hell as they please. Bring as many as you can, trying to save the best, and come on. A band of Gro' Vont' is going to meet us at Wolf Point. So I aim to drive north along the Prairie Elk. The two pairs of you working northeast and northwest can just as well start picking up cattle as you leave here, and push ’em along as you go.”

“What you want done if we run into Lasham’s riders?”

“I figure they’ll be holed in until the snow lets up, but if it turns clear, and you run into ’em, quit your cattle and circle back. What I want now is cattle, not war. You’ll hear plenty of lead whispering ‘cousin’ before you’re through!”

They slept that night under the slowly falling snow. Roper himself made coffee and routed out his riders two hours before the first light. They caught their horses in the dark, with hands that fumbled the stiffened ropes, then split off in pairs to comb the range.

Roper left one man to hold the horses where they could be found again and scouted southeast alone to look for signs of activity at Lasham’s camp. A curl of sulky smoke hung over the little shanty by the corrals, but no one was working, so far as he could make out. He found himself badly tempted to go into the camp, posing as a wandering stranger, and see what he could learn from Lasham’s winter foreman, but concluded that he could risk no gunfight now.

For two days, Roper watched the enemy camp while the snow held on, piling a deeper and deeper mat. Then on the third day, he returned to the rendezvous as the roundup men began straggling in.

Tex Long was the first one back.

"This range is plumb solid with stock," Tex declared. "How many head do you figure me and Kid Johnson scraped up, just us two?"

"Well," Roper grunted, "upwards of a dozen—I should hope."

"Better'n six hundred head! Lord Almighty, Bill! Figuring they're worth twenty dollars apiece and allowing that all the other boys do as good, we're liable to get out of here with around eighty thousand dollars' worth of cattle! You realize that?"

"We're not out of here yet. The weather's breaking, Tex."

"Let her break! Only thing bothers me, ain't those Gro' Vont' going to be awful spooky about coming down so close to Fort Union?"

"They aren't worse scared than hungry, I guess."

Tex Long couldn't understand Bill Roper's grim lack of enthusiasm. "Can't you get it through your head, kid? We're punishing hell out of him!"

"I'm thinking of something else," Bill Roper said. "I'm thinking of a dead man under a pile of stone, south out of Ogallala."

That was only a half truth. More than he was thinking of Dusty King, Roper was thinking of the letter in his pocket—the appeal of a girl who needed him in some unknown way, and who did not even know why he couldn't come.

All the next day, they worked to throw the little bunches together into a trail herd. Not all of them had done as well as Tex Long and Kid Johnson, but most of them had done well enough. And then, at last, the first herd privateered in the Great Raid began to roll. A long unsteadily-moving river of cattle poured northward, a dark welter in the thinning fall of the snow. White-faces, mostly, blocky and heavy, well wintered on the prairie hay—Roper counted two thousand six hundred odd!

"Git on, you dogies—move up, move up!"

Pressed hard by the heavy force of cowboys, the cattle bawled and complained but humped along northward into the valley of the Prairie Elk, leading out on their last long trail.

Rounding up within a day's ride of Miles City itself, Roper's men had taken this herd almost out of the very corrals of Lasham's outposts, and yet, so far as any of them knew, that swift-moving drive represented a harder blow than had ever been struck a cattleman in a single raid. In all their months of effort, the winter wild bunch had been unable to achieve an equal reprisal upon Lasham, and now they could hardly believe their own success. They forced the cattle hard, driving through the clogging snow at a rate incredible to men accustomed to handling market herds.

"Roll along, roll along! Hup, Babe, hup!"

The cattle that broke the way through the snow kept dropping back, blown and tired, but as fast as they failed, others were forced forward to take their places. Long-horned, stag-legged steers of the old Texas strain fought the riders, breaking the heavy column repeatedly in their wild-eyed thrusts for liberty, and these were allowed to get away. Gaunt, weak cattle lagged back, unable to keep up even under the snapping rope ends of the tail riders. They were also allowed to drop out, promptly forgotten. Yet, in that first day, the side riders swept in enough north-roaming cattle to more than make up the loss. Tex Long, wearing out ponies to do the work of six men, was singing a trail song more exultantly than it had ever been sung before.

"Roll, dogies, roll! Git on, git on!"

Thus, the first herd to fall to the Great Raid plowed northward, the backs of the hard-driven cattle steaming northward across the tributaries of Timber Creek and the Little Dry, northward still beyond the valley of the Prairie Elk, gone, clean gone, out of Lasham's range. Their work had been bitterly hard in the smother of the snow, but their first slashing blow had met with an unbelievable success.

"Hump, you cow critters! Turn him, boy!"

Roper went with the herd as far as Circle Horse Creek, but when they had forded the shallows, crashing through the rotten ice, he turned back. With him, he took four men who he believed would do what he said. The cattle were moving more slowly now, plodding doggedly through the heavy going. Tex Long and the remaining eight men could hold them to their way. What was needed now was work of a different kind, and Roper thought he knew how that was to be done.

It was his intention to fight a rear guard action—not only for this first herd, which would be delivered within the week to the Indians who would spirit it away, but for the protection of all the rest of the wild bunch raiding westward.

But now, as he neared the head of the Little Dry, a rider came dropping down a long slope upon a racing horse. His carbine was held above his ragged sombrero in a sign of peace, and as he came near, they saw that it was Hat Crick Tommy.

Roper jumped his horse out to meet Hat Crick. "What is it? Is there any word? Did she—"

Tommy's face was haggard with fatigue. "She's gone!" he jerked out. "She's been to Miles City—and now she's gone!"

"Gone? Gone where?"

"Nobody knows. She's missing—disappeared—strayed or lost or rustled, God knows which! Her father's wild-crazy, and every K-G outfit in the north is combing the trails—"

Roper sat staring for a full half minute. Then his hands fumbled for his reata and shook out the loop.

"Turn that roan pony! I've got to have a fresh horse . . ."

CHAPTER TWENTY-ONE

Shoshone Wilce, riding with Jody Gordon through the same hundred-mile snow which screened Bill Roper and Tex Long in their raid on the Little Dry, found himself the most bewildered and the most unhappy of men.

In a way, he sympathized with Jody's purpose—insofar as he understood it. But what stood out a good deal more plainly in his thoughts was that his luck was putting him in wrong with some very rough-acting people. Shoshone saw with great clarity that he had every chance of getting himself shot.

He could have refused to guide Jody Gordon to Bill Roper's rendezvous; he thought it improbable that Jody Gordon would have been able to locate the rendezvous alone. But whether she found it, or merely got herself lost, Shoshone Wilce would have been answerable to Bill Roper for leaving her to attempt the ride alone. And he supposed that Roper, now accredited as one of the most dangerous and unrelenting gunfighters on the Plains, would be hot on his trail.

The alternative he had chosen offered no greater prospect for a long and helpful life. Lew Gordon would go wild as a wounded silvertip at the disappearance of his daughter, and every

King-Gordon cowboy in the country would be scouring the brakes after Shoshone's scalp. The situation would have looked better to him if he had seen any hope of Jody's succeeding in getting Bill Roper and her father together.

"You'll never get anywheres with it," he kept objecting to Jody. "I'd just as leave try to hitch up a bobcat and a longhorn steer, and drive 'em in team, as try to get your Paw and Bill Roper together."

"I can try. I have to try."

For Jody believed now that the split between Lew Gordon and Bill Roper was the basis of inconceivable disaster—not only immediate and personal, but far-reaching in its import to the cow country. Together, those two very different cattlemen could have beaten Thorpe and consolidated the King-Gordon empire. Bill Roper could have been built into another Dusty King, supplying the bold, hard-fighting, but practical qualities that Dusty King had meant to the partnership of King-Gordon. Without Dusty King—or Bill Roper in Dusty King's place—Jody Gordon felt that King-Gordon was incomplete, unfitted to survive the times. Instead of settling its vast foundations into a sound structure that would steady the whole cow country, King-Gordon would go down, carrying many lesser cattle companies with it, injuring the cow country throughout the length of the Plains.

Separated, Lew Gordon and Bill Roper were mutually destructive. Lew Gordon was probably right that Bill Roper's savage attacks upon the Thorpe interests were the cause of Ben Thorpe's heavy reprisals upon King-Gordon. And even though Roper might bring down Ben Thorpe in the end, which still seemed incredible, he could never profit by his victory, even if he lived. Unless Gordon and Roper could be reconciled, Roper would in the end become just one more outlawed cowboy whose trails could have no meaning and only one end.

Jody Gordon had one other motive in attempting the all but hopeless reconciliation. She believed her father's life to be in the sharpest danger. Bill Roper, an even harder fighter than the old trail breaker who had trained him, would automatically take those precautions that would safeguard her father's life, if once they could be brought to work together again.

But the first move toward reconciliation must come from Bill Roper himself. If she could persuade Roper to this, there was a bare possibility that she could also manage her father. It was a forlorn hope, but, as she saw it, of such vital importance that it could no longer be ignored. It was as if events that would alter the whole history of the cow country lay in her persuasion of those two stubborn men. She rode doggedly now, with set face, trusting Shoshone to find the way.

They rode until after midnight, blind, as far as Jody could see, in the wet fall of the snow. They threw down their bedrolls then in the shelter of stunted snow-laden trees, and Shoshone Wilce measured grain for the horses onto his own poncho.

"They'll never follow the trail I've twisted out—not with the snow favoring us like it does," Shoshone suggested hopefully. "We've lost considerable time, foxing up the trail, but it would be awful unlucky for me if we was caught up with."

"I know."

They pushed on again, miserable in the raw dawn, after coffee which Shoshone made in a frying pan. All day long, they rode steadily, stopping only once for bread and bacon and to bolster their horses with more grain. They were moving through a country now which Jody had never seen, a country broken and rolling with long weather breaks of scraggly timber. Twice they sighted distant smoke, pressed low by the leaden sky. Watchful and worried, Shoshone gave these signs of encampment a wide berth.

The snow slacked off, giving place to a bitter wind. Jody's knees stiffened with saddle cramp, and she continually had to nurse her fingers deep in her pockets to keep them from going numb. She had a strange sense of having taken an irrevocable step which she might find great reason to regret. The fact that the snow had hidden the trail they had made so that no one could follow to find her gave her a feeling of being cut off from everything friendly she had ever known. She no longer knew where she was. She set her eyes straight ahead, too proud to ask Shoshone how far they had come, or how much farther they must go.

Just before dusk, they climbed a long rocky ridge that commanded the length of a shallow valley set brokenly with juniper and ragged cedar.

Shoshone motioned her to stop her horse. "Wait a minute."

Far down the valley, Jody Gordon could see a faint haze that blurred the rabbit-fur gray and brown of the brush and runty timber. A whisky-jack cried mournfully for a time somewhere in the scrub while Shoshone Wilce sat motionless upon his tired horse, but this sound had stopped before Shoshone finished his study of the valley.

"That's smoke," Shoshone Wilce said at last. "This ought to be the place."

"So we really got here at last . . ."

"Two hours more."

"The smoke—that means he's there."

Shoshone Wilce, suspicious and doubtful by temperament, was less sure. "Don't know if it's him. Somebody's there. Or, anyway, somebody's been there."

He shivered, rubbed his nose with his glove, and led off down the slope.

Night overtook them as they threaded the long valley. Just as darkness closed, a great horned owl dodged in front of them, winging silently close to the snow, a drifting shadow, but though it passed almost under their horses' feet, the tired ponies did not shy. To Jody in her weariness, it seemed that they plodded on and on while the prophesied two hours stretched at least to four. She had almost given up ever reaching the end of the trail at all when Shoshone Wilce spoke at last, low-voiced.

"I kin smell the cooking smoke."

"Good."

"I hope so. I don't know this country like I wish I did."

A swift panic chilled Jody at the thought of meeting Bill Roper face to face again after so long a time. She tried to imagine what she was going to say to him and was completely unable. She wondered how he would look, and whether he would be glad to see her.

Now, Shoshone Wilce reached out to catch her bridle reins, and they stopped. She started to ask what the matter was, but checked herself. Wilce had become tensely watchful, and she saw that he was listening.

After a moment or two of utter stillness, Wilce whispered, "Wait a minute," and pushed his horse slowly forward into the dark. For a little while as he moved away from her, she could see the tall black silhouette of his horse against the pale snow, but soon this blurred with the darkness and was lost. Just after she lost sight of him altogether, she heard his pony's hoofs fall silent as if he had stopped again, and there was a long interval while nothing happened, and she heard no sound except the low thin voice of the wind across the snow-laden brush and the rhythmic breathing of her own pony.

Growing impatient at last, and a little uneasy, Jody moved her pony ahead after Shoshone. There was a moment or two of panic, in which it seemed that she had lost him altogether in the dark, but her pony knew where the other was if she did not, and presently brought her alongside.

Shoshone Wilce was sitting perfectly motionless on his horse, staring ahead into a darkness to which the snow gave a curiously deceptive luminosity that did not aid the eye.

"That's her, all right," Shoshone whispered at last.

Straining her eyes, Jody could not see what he was looking at.

"I don't like this so good," Shoshone said.

"What's the matter?"

"No lights."

"Maybe there's no window on this side."

"Otter be."

"You mean you think—"

"Shut up."

They moved ahead a little now, Jody holding her pony beside that of Shoshone Wilce. Shoshone moved his horse forward twenty paces, and stopped again for a full minute, then ten paces more.

Jody said, "What in the world—"

Wilce seized her arm and silenced her with a quick shake. Then suddenly—

An inarticulate oath snarled in Shoshone's throat. He snatched at Jody's rein, whirling her pony around. His own horse came straight up on its hind legs as he spun it at close quarters.

"Get going!" he said between his teeth and brought his romal down across her pony's flank in a snapping cut that made it plunge ahead. She heard the rip of steel on leather as Shoshone's gun came out. Then the silence of the night exploded into happenings that were incredible.

Two guns smashed out in a swift flurry of detonation. A queer whistling grunt was knocked out of Jody's horse. It dropped from under her, and the ground struck upward with stunning violence.

For a moment, Jody Gordon lay motionless, her cheek buried in the cool snow. She was aware of further firing, and more than one running horse, and she tasted blood from a cut lip, but at first, she was unable to think.

After a moment, as she raised herself, she could make out figures that seemed all around her, although there were only two or three. Her hair had fallen loose about her shoulders, blowing into her mouth and eyes, and she struck it aside.

Someone said, "Well, we got one of 'em, anyway."

"Haul him inside."

"Look out now, Bud—no funny business." The voice was unknown to her, as was the figure that now bent over her. Suddenly, the man jerked forward to peer at her more closely.

"Jesus—what the—Hey! It's Calamity Jane, or somebody!"

Jody Gordon struggled to her feet, shock giving way to anger. "You fools, are you crazy? Bill Roper will kill you for this!"

There was a moment's silence, and she sensed rather than saw that they were looking at each other.

"Bill Roper," one of them repeated. "She says she's looking for Bill Roper!"

"Lady, you better come inside!"

CHAPTER TWENTY-TWO

Dazed and shaky as the fall of her killed horse had left her, Jody Gordon still appeared the most self-possessed of them all as she allowed herself to be led into the little cabin at which she had hoped to find Bill Roper. Her boots were silent on the hard-tramped bare earth of the floor, but the clean blue steel of her spurs rang thinly as she turned to face the two men who followed her.

The shack in which she now found herself was a cramped makeshift, intended only as a shelter for cowboys, storm-caught while riding the northern limits of the Fork Creek range. Nobody had had a stove to waste on this place, nor the ambition to haul one here, but a shallow recess of stones and sods served as a fireplace, filling the little room with an unnecessary heat. A single lantern hung from a roof pole, and now, by its yellow light, the two men studied her with an unconcealed amazement.

"By God," said the older of the two, "it's a girl, all right!"

In the dull lantern glow, this man's eyes were of an indeterminate greenish color, but sharply clear, and steady as stone in a bony, almost emaciated face. His voice trailed off now as if sheer wonderment had taken away his breath. "It sure is! Yes, sir, it sure—"

The other man, tall enough so that the door at his back looked small, was much the younger of the two. His face was prematurely hard-cut—the face of a man who even in youth had learned an effectiveness in action upon which he could well rely. He spoke sharply.

"Jim—you know who this is?"

The older man's eyes rested steadily upon Jody's face, sober and impartial. "Seems like I seen her before," he decided. "Can't seem to place her, though. She's a good looker, all right, ain't she?"

"This is a hell of a time to be thinking about that," the other said edgily. "Jim, that's Lew Gordon's girl!"

"Good Lord Almighty! I believe you're right!"

"It's her, sure enough!"

"Just don't seem possible she'd be—"

"Ain't possible. But—it's her!"

"So you know me?" Jody said.

"I seen you once in Ogallala, and another time in Bandera."

The older man shifted his eyes to his partner. He had a trick of moving his eyes sharply without moving his head, and it gave him a curious aspect of listening keenly—listening with the complete attentiveness of an animal whose whole business of life depends upon the sharpness of its senses.

"Damnedest queer turn of the cards," he said, "I ever seen in all my born days!"

The younger man's voice was sharp and strained. "Jim, we got to get her out of here and get her out quick!"

The man called Jim appeared to consider intently, his eyes still on the other's face. "I ain't so sure," he said after a moment.

"Then you better get sure," the hard-faced youngster said impatiently. "We had a mighty sweet setup here—until she horned in. The quicker we get her out of here—"

"I ain't so sure it ain't sweeter now," the older man said slowly. He had the assurance of one who knows his decisions will hold good. Undoubtedly, he was the leader here. "I was just thinking . . ."

"Well?" Jody prompted him.

She stood straight and still, her hands in the pockets of her sheepskin. In this unexpected environment, her face looked extraordinarily sensitive and delicate, framed in the soft tumble of her hair, but it was as expressionless as any cowboy's could have been, and her eyes were dark and cool.

"You talk like a fool," the younger man snapped at his superior. "Look what we got! We got the law back of us. We got the most powerful cowman in the West back of us. We got one of the biggest rewards that's ever been hung up, right ready to drop into our hands. We've located Roper's main shebang after working on it for months. We got all the odds in the world in our favor—and here comes this girl and bogs the whole works!"

"Just how do you figure she bogs it?"

"We got every chance of nailing our man, right here, any hour now. But don't ever think we'll nail him without a hell of a sharp fight. Suppose this girl gets hurt in this fight, or gets loose and loses herself, or runs out of luck some other way?"

"Can't see as we owe nothing to Lew Gordon, or any of his kin," the older man said grimly.

"What the hell has that got to do with it? This girl's old man is known the whole length of the Trail. What happens to us if she gets herself in a bind, and it's blamed on us? Every backing we got will drop out from under us like a shot pony—Ben Thorpe, first of all. Half the West'll be out to hang us higher'n a buzzard, and the reward goes to hell in a whoop!"

"I see that, all right."

"You sure by God better see it! This is plumb poison, Jim. There ain't a girl the length of the Trail whose name is better known, or who'd work out worse medicine for us if anything went wrong. The quicker we get her out of here—"

"Can't."

"What's the reason we can't?"

"We got the bear by the tail. She's dynamite so long as she's here. I grant you that. But what if we let her go? She warns Roper off. Then where are we?"

Jody Gordon's throat constricted. Lots of cowmen were named Jim. But now suddenly, she knew who the older of the two men must be.

"You know," she said slowly, "I believe I remember you, now."

"Why, it hardly seems likely that—"

"You're Jim Leathers," Jody said.

Once more, there was repeated the exchange of glances between the two men. Then the older shrugged.

"I guess you're right," he admitted. "I guess that's my name."

She knew well enough who Jim Leathers was. She didn't know how he'd first got started on the trail that had led him through the smoke of so many guns and given him a record which put him on a par with such famous gunfighters as Hat Crick Tommy and Tex Long. But one fact stood out clear and definite—Jim Leathers had been a Ben Thorpe man always—gunfighter, night rider, leader of warrior outfits for Ben Thorpe.

And knowing who their leader was, she could no longer doubt why these men were here. Already, the belief was all up and down the Trail that it was Bill Roper who was harrying the Thorpe herds under Lasham in Montana. Men were saying that his raiders moved in and out upon the Lasham herds like wolves, inflicting damage against which the Lasham riders seemed helpless. Small wonder if Thorpe had sent these picked fighting men—perhaps with the badges of deputy United States Marshals, for all she knew—to comb the north for the hard-riding outlaw leader, with orders to rub him out at all costs.

"Of course," Jim Leathers said to Jody, "we never would have blazed out at you the way we did, if we'd known who you was."

Jody's head had cleared now from the dazed shock of the gun action and the smash-down she had received from the fall of her horse, and she angered.

"It seems to me you blaze out mighty free without knowing who you throw down on!"

"Well, you know—the truth is—we was expecting somebody else."

"You were expecting Bill Roper," Jody said. "Naturally, you'd rather bushwhack him in the dark than risk his gun, wouldn't you? Well, you're wasting your time. This was Roper's camp once—it evidently isn't now. You ought to know by this time that he camps only a little while in one place. And if you mean to wait until Roper rides into a trap like this—you'll wait a long, long time!"

Except for a perfunctory glance, the men

appeared to ignore her. "When we picked her up," Jim Leathers asked his partner, "what was it that she said? Didn't she use Bill Roper's name?"

"I didn't catch it all. Something about Bill Roper would sure get us for drilling her horse."

The two men stared at each other for a long moment, oddly preoccupied, as if each sought in the other the answer to an unspoken question.

Jim Leathers's jaw muscles contracted so that the slanting light of the lantern outlined a flat lump of tobacco in his cheek.

"Once," he said, "I heard that Roper and Lew Gordon come mighty close to a bust-up on account of Gordon's girl. Some folks thought they did bust up. Do you guess—could it just happen to be that—"

The eyes of both men shifted to Jody's face. Behind Jim Leathers, the shadows from the fire were diluted by the lantern light so that they appeared the half-seen ghosts of shadows, but they weaved and shifted in a wavering phantasm. In all that room, only Jim Leathers's eyes seemed completely steady. They had turned as frigidly metallic as any ore that ever came out of the rock-bound hills. Jody had a creepy feeling that animals were staring at her.

"What time," he asked, "were you expecting Bill Roper?"

"I have no reason to expect him at all," Jody said.

The younger man's eyes were keen with a repressed excitement. "Jim—you figure she come to meet Bill Roper here?"

"She didn't come here by accident," Leathers said with conviction, "any more than you or me. And she sure didn't come here to throw in with us."

"But, God, Jim—if she's run off from her old man to throw in with Roper, then it must be that Gordon ain't backing Roper, after all! Why should she come gallivanting clear out here if Gordon and Roper are hand in glove? We always thought—"

"That's no bother of mine," Leathers said. "Roper's the man I want." His voice turned soft and happy. "Just kind of begins to look like I'm going to get him!" He turned sharply on Jody. "You can just as well speak your piece. We'll get the whole story, anyway, when the boys bring your side rider in. He'll talk, all right, before we're through!"

"You'll learn nothing from him," Jody said. "If he didn't get clear, I have no doubt he's dead. You'll never take him alive—that I know."

Jim Leathers grinned a little. It did not improve his looks. "Suppose they bring him in only about half alive?" he suggested. His tone changed as he added, "Of course, as for me, I'm sure hoping he got away."

A swift panic struck Jody with the shock of

a blow to the face. If Jim Leathers wished, he could hold her here—literally as bait with which to draw the man whom it was his mission to kill. If Shoshone Wilce had gotten clear and could reach Roper, Roper would certainly attack as soon as the best ponies of the raiders could bring him. Or, failing to locate Roper, Shoshone Wilce might even bring her father—and what orders Jim Leathers had in regard to Lew Gordon she could only surmise.

"I'm getting sick of this," Jody told Jim Leathers. "You owe me a horse; there can't possibly be any argument about that. I'll have to ask you to rope a pony and bring him to my saddle—and I'll be on my way!"

"Awful bad job, catching up these Sioux country ponies in the dark."

"For more than five years," Jody said, "neither you nor your men have camped out the night without ponies waiting under saddle. Right now, you've got caught-up ponies standing outside. You owe one of them to me."

Jim Leathers spoke mildly, measuring his words. "You've rode a long way in the cold," he said. "The boys'll get you some coffee and grub, and bring your bedroll in. I guess you better figure to stop for the night." He grinned again, not reassuringly. "We're a little crowded here, and maybe not so stylish as you're used to, but that ain't going to hurt you none."

“I don’t want your coffee, and you know it,” Jody said.

Leathers ignored that. “Who was this side rider of yours?” he demanded.

“You’ll learn nothing from me—neither that nor anything else. I’ll take a pony—and I’ll take it now!”

Slowly, Leathers shook his head.

“You won’t give me a pony?”

“I’m afraid—you’ll have to wait until your friends come, lady.”

For Jody Gordon’s white flash of anger, there was no outlet whatever. She turned away to hide from them the furious tears that sprang into her eyes. She took off her sheepskin coat and flung it on the table, for the room was very hot, but because her fingers were still chilled to the bone, she pulled off her gloves, tucked them into her belt, and went to the shallow fireplace to hold out her hands to the flames.

The two men watched her with detached admiration. Her slim figure was clad in the rough blue clothes the range riders wore, but the firelight glinted from silver belt conchos which were carved with intricate traceries, and her boots were the finest that money could cause to be made. Neither of the men had ever seen anything stranger than this girl’s presence here.

“Damnedest deal of cards I ever saw in all my born days,” the younger man marveled again.

"It's happened before. Some rattle-head girl is always running off after some saddle tramp. This time it's just a lucky turn for us, that's all."

Their voices were low but not so low that Jody could not easily hear what they said. They were discussing her as if she were a horse.

"You're wasting your time," Jody Gordon tossed over her shoulder. She knew well enough that no argument could be of any avail against Jim Leathers, that practiced killer, with his casual, deceptive voice and his sharp and perceiving eyes, but she had to try. "I don't know where Bill Roper is any more than you do, and neither does my side rider. And Bill Roper doesn't know I'm here."

They did not answer her, but their silence implied disbelief, and she spoke again.

"It's true that I came here looking for Bill Roper," she said. "I had my own reasons for that, and what you think about it doesn't matter to me in the least. But evidently, he isn't here, and I don't know anything more about it than that. The quicker you give me a horse, the better it's likely to be for you. Range war or no range war, there still is a general opinion among a whole lot of people as to how Lew Gordon's daughter is to be treated on the range. I don't think it will bring you any luck to go against that, any more than anybody else."

Leathers made no comment. Obviously he

had no way of testing the truth of what she said except to wait and see if Roper appeared.

They went on talking now in the drawling, well-considered speech of the trail, long pauses marking every interchange. Whatever else they might think of her, they evidently did not consider that she implied any necessity to secrecy.

"Do you reckon," the younger man suggested, "that rider couldn't've been Bill Roper himself?"

Jim Leathers was contemptuous. "Bill Roper would have stood his ground. He sure would never have run off and left the girl with her horse down. Might be it was some little squirt of a King-Gordon cowboy. There's always plenty of weak-minded little mutts that some girl like this can wrap around her finger—even up to taking 'em to another man. But more likely it was a Roper man, and if he's alive, he'll bring Bill Roper here—if he ain't already on his way."

"If Roper is on his way," the younger rider said thoughtfully, "and this side rider of hers has got loose and meets him, so that Roper knows what he's up against—that might be kind of bad medicine, Jim. If he's got his war-riders with him—"

"I've missed hooking up with Roper twenty times when I thought I had him," Leathers said. "I'd sooner meet up with him on any terms than carry back the word that I fell down."

A shiver ran the length of Jody Gordon's body.

Casually, as if they were talking about getting breakfast, these quiet-faced men were speaking of a proposed death—the death of a boy who had once been very close to her, and very dear. Suddenly, she was able to glimpse the power and the depth of the animosity behind the mission of these men. No effort and no cost would seem to Ben Thorpe too great if, in the end, Bill Roper was struck out of existence.

Behind that vast malignance was reason enough. The Texas Rustlers' War, still fresh in everyone's minds, had not only placed Thorpe in definite hazard of financial collapse, it had been a crushing humiliation as well. In his war upon Tanner in Texas, Roper had accomplished what all men had called impossible. But now, inevitably, there rose against Roper all the outraged power that Thorpe controlled; a relentless and implacable hunt-down that could only end with Roper's death—or the destruction of Ben Thorpe himself. The band of killers into whose ambush Jody had ridden was undoubtedly only one of several, already in the field. Later there would be more, and more, until the day should come when there would no longer be any place for Roper's raiders to turn . . .

She thought, "If only I could have found him in time . . . If only I could have got him back into King-Gordon . . . I could have got him back into King-Gordon."

"Jim," the younger rider said soberly, "if Roper's got his wild bunch with him—Jim, it's such a fight as none of us have ever gone into yet! When you stop to think that any time—any minute—a bunch of 'em may land in here—"

"Charley's on lookout," Jim Leathers shrugged. "We'll know in plenty of time."

A silence fell, a long silence. Heavy upon Jody Gordon was the panic of an open-space creature held helpless within close walls. Her voice was low and bitter. "You're set on holding me here?"

To answer her, Jim Leathers seemed to have to rouse himself. It was as if his thoughts had run ahead, deep into the next forty-eight hours, perhaps living in the smoke of expected guns.

"No call to put it that way," he said mildly, almost gently. But his eyes denied that mildness, so that behind him Jody sensed again the vast animosity built by the Texas Rustlers' War—the malevolent power for which this man was only a cutting edge.

"I want a flat answer," Jody said. "Are you going to give me a horse, or not?"

Once more, Jim Leathers's canine teeth showed in his peculiarly unpleasant grin. "Hell, no," he said.

CHAPTER TWENTY-THREE

Perhaps Lew Gordon should have known that if Bill Roper learned of Jody's disappearance at all, Roper would come directly to him. And, knowing this, he should have prepared himself. But Lew Gordon had not met Roper face to face in nearly two years, and nothing was farther from his mind than the possibility that Roper would walk in upon him now.

Upon this night, Lew Gordon was pacing the main room of his little Miles City house. Forty-eight hours had passed since his daughter's disappearance and the old cattleman, haggard from the effect of a sleepless night upon a physique no longer young, had lashed himself into a state of repressed fury comparable to that of a trap-baffled mountain lion, or a goaded bear. Everything that could be done to locate his daughter was being done; the strong King-Gordon outfits in Montana had thrown aside all other work, that every available rider might be devoted to the job of tracing out every imaginable possibility. The complete failure of his organization to learn anything whatsoever chafed Gordon as a saddle galls a raw-backed bronc.

He knew that Jody's disappearance was voluntary, and he knew its purpose. The brief but highly informative note that Jody had left him told him that much. It simply said:

> "One of you must be made to see reason. I am going to talk to Billy Roper myself."

What this did not tell him was where Roper was, or how Jody expected to find him. Impatient of mystery and delay, he could not understand why his many far-scattered cowboys could dig up no word. He neither believed Jody competent to travel the Montana ranges alone, nor trusted any rider who might have been with her. On top of that, he had made certain that all of his own men were accounted for and could not imagine who was acting as Jody's guide—if anyone was—unless it might be a Roper man. For all he knew, his daughter was by this time lost somewhere in the frozen wastes of snow, in immediate desperate need of help.

A constant but irregular chain of couriers kept coming in to him from his outlying outfits, a messenger system that brought him little comfort, but enabled him to direct operations. Tonight, it was a little after eight o'clock as the latest of these riders came in from one of the western camps.

This was an ineffectual youngster on the payrolls as a horse wrangler; he brought word that nothing had been accomplished, and Gordon practically skinned him alive.

"Get back to your worthless outfit," Lew Gordon finished at last. "Get a fresh horse and let me hear later that you burnt up the trail. By God, I'm sick of this infernal dawdling! Get out! Get out of my sight!"

At quarter after nine, the town marshal came in, a lank, weary-looking man, trailing a couple of his deputies at his heels. This man brought the first word of any kind that Gordon had received yet.

"We've kept right on checking up on everybody in town," the marshal reported, "and we finally found a teamster off a hide wagon that thinks he seen her ride out of town. He says he met her in the road as he was coming into town with his team, just after dark night before last."

"Alone?" Gordon demanded. "Was she alone?"

"She was riding with a man."

"Who was it? What kind of looking man?"

"He doesn't know that. You see, it was dark, and all he can say is it didn't look like anybody he knew. The girl was on a good lively-stepping horse. Leastwise he's virtually certain it was a girl. But he says he didn't know the horse. They was heading out of town toward the west, and there was blanket rolls and saddle bags on both saddles."

"Is that all you got?"

"That's all we got yet. As soon as we found out this, we thought you'd want to hear it. We aim to try again on the horse situation, next thing. If we can only find out whose horses those were, we'll find out who the man with her was."

"It beats me," Lew Gordon exploded impatiently, "why the hell you can't find out a simple thing like what horses she took. I know hootin' well she didn't take mine, and somebody sure must know—"

"It's awful hard going, finding out that," the marshal said mildly. "What few friends this Roper has in Miles City seem real tie-fast. If they're close enough to Roper to know what he's up to, they're close enough to keep their mouth shut. Mostly, they're old sidekicks of Dusty King's. Dusty was a great hand to make friends that never would go back on him, and it seems like they don't go back on his boy, neither."

Lew Gordon suppressed his exasperation with the greatest difficulty, but he did not speak again until he had it under control.

"All right," he said at last. "I guess you fellers are doing the best you can. Go on ahead, try to find out about the ponies they took, and who she was with—in case that was really her."

When they were gone, Lew Gordon sat alone for a little while. For the moment, his helpless anger was burned down into a heavy weariness. His mind was full of his daughter, whom he persistently pictured as a little girl, much more of a child than she actually was anymore.

Suddenly, it struck him how curious it was that in this bare room in which he sat, there was no sign of any kind that Jody had ever been here at all. This was partly because she had never lived here nor even been expected here, but it brought home to him sharply how much of his life had been given to cattle, how little to his daughter. All around him was a sparse disorder of saddles, blankets, ropes, and guns, and a great litter of business papers. There were spurs, and boots, bridles, tally books, and the irons of his various brands, but not one single thing to indicate that a little motherless girl had ever claimed any part of his thought. It made him realize how little he knew his daughter, and how little he had ever given her of himself.

This was Lew Gordon's state of mind as the door thrust open, letting in a brief lash of wintry wind, and he wheeled in his chair to face the last man on earth he had expected to see.

Bill Roper shook a powdering of dry snow off the roll of his coat collar, then stood looking at Lew Gordon in a cool, hard silence as he pulled off his gloves. This was the outlaw leader on whose head Gordon had put a price double that posted by Thorpe, his own bitterest enemy. Once this man had been almost a son to Lew Gordon—the adopted son, in actuality, of Lew Gordon's dead partner. But a definite enmity now replaced what a little while ago had been a friendship as deep and close as the variance in their ages could permit. All the meaning of their association, almost as long as Bill Roper's life, was gone, wiped out by those two smoky years since the death of Dusty King.

For a moment or two, Lew Gordon stared at him in utter disbelief. Then he whipped to his feet.

"Where is she?" he demanded intensely, furiously. "What have you done with her?"

Bill Roper no longer looked like the youngster Dusty King had raised on the trail. His gray eyes looked hard and extremely competent, old beyond his age, in a face so dark and lean-carved it was hard to recognize behind it the face of Dusty King's kid. He made no attempt to answer a question that was necessarily meaningless to him. He finished pulling off his gloves, unbuttoned his coat, and hooked his thumbs in his belt before he spoke.

"I heard yesterday that Jody has turned up missing," he said. "I came to Miles hell-for-leather to see if it's so. From what I could find out down in the town, no word has come in on where she is. If that's true, I don't aim to give my time to anything else until she's found."

"By God," said Lew Gordon, "I've got reason to think you know exactly where she is right now!"

"If I knew that, I wouldn't be here. What I want from you is what you know about this."

"You mean to deny you know where she is?" Gordon shouted.

Roper's voice did not change. "You talk like a fool," he said.

Lew Gordon's eyes were savagely intent upon Roper's face; he was trying to discover if this man could be believed.

"You may be lying," he added at last, "and you may not, but I'll tell you this—you sure won't leave here till I find out where my girl is. You're wanted anyway, my laddie buck. There's a legal reward on your head, right now—and part of it was put up by me."

"I heard that," Bill Roper said. "When I get ready to leave, I'll leave, all right. My advice to you is to begin using your head. I may be in a kind of funny position. But it puts me where I know things about the Montana range that neither you nor your outfits have got any clue to. If you want your daughter back, you better figure out how to use what I know about the Deep Grass."

Lew Gordon compelled himself to temporize. What he couldn't get around was his own belief that Roper knew something definite, specific, about where Jody had gone—or had started out to go. He must have known also, in spite of the bluff to which anger had prompted him, that he could not hold Roper here when Roper decided to leave, nor force any information from him in any way whatever.

"What is it you want to know?" he asked at last, helpless, and angry in his helplessness.

"In the first place, I want to know what made you think Jody was with me?"

"You swear," Lew Gordon demanded, "you don't know the answer to that?"

"I don't swear anything," Roper said. "I asked you a question, Lew."

Lew Gordon hesitated. It was a good many years since anyone had talked to him in the tone Bill Roper took, but for once, the purpose in hand out-powered the violence of his natural reaction. He turned from his litter of papers and handed Bill Roper the little scrap of Jody's handwriting, which was all she had left to indicate where she was gone.

"One of you must be made to reason. I am going to talk to Billy Roper myself."

When Bill Roper had read that, the eyes of the two men met in hostile question.

"This looks mighty like a false lead, to me," Bill Roper said at last. "Like as if she aimed to cover up where she really went. Don't hardly seem likely she'd start out to come to me."

"My girl don't cover up anything," Lew Gordon snarled at him.

"You lost her, didn't you?"

Gordon turned away with a jerk. His boot heels

sounded dull and heavy on the carpetless floor as he resumed the pacing which had lately occupied so many of his hours.

"She in love with some man?" Roper demanded bluntly.

Lew Gordon reddened darkly, but he answered. "Hell, no."

"Some boy in one of your outfits could be shining up to her without you knowing it, I guess."

"All my boys are accounted for. She didn't even know anybody else, anywhere around Miles."

"She rode out with somebody just the same."

Gordon's eyes lifted sharply. "You knew that?"

"Seem to, don't I?"

Gordon resumed his sullen pacing.

"Lew," Roper said, an edge of anger coming into his own voice, "did you have a row with that girl?"

"Stay back of your rights," Gordon warned him. "There's such a thing as more slack than I'll take from anybody."

"Uh-huh," Roper said, "you did have a row with her. Just what was this about, Lew?"

Suddenly, the older man came to the end of his endurance. "By God, if anything came up between Jody and me, you were behind it! Just as you're the cause of the cutthroat war that Thorpe has put on us in every territory in the West, and every mile of the Trail. Just as you're the cause of every costly ruckus King-Gordon has had since the death of Dusty King. It's a wonder to me I don't blast you where you stand."

"Even if I stood here and let you," Roper commented, "you couldn't fire on me while I stood here without raising a hand. You've proved out mighty weak-handed, Lew, without Dusty King, and mighty short of memory, and general guts, but you couldn't ever bring yourself to that."

Gordon's speech was thick-tongued with repression, but his voice was low. "I've stood for peace and law and decency; you've turned yourself over to cow-stealing and bushwhacking and gunplay. You've started things no mortal man can stop, gone so deep that you can't ever back up. So deep that you can't ever get square with the world again, or your record forgot."

"Mostly," Bill said, "I've stood for the memory of a man. But let that go. What I want from you is why you had a row with Jody—and why she should come hunting for me, if that's what she did."

"I know she went looking for you because she said she did. My girl don't lie."

Roper shrugged. "Why in all hell should she do that?"

"It was your own man talked her into it," Gordon said with menace.

"My own man? What man?"

"A man of yours sneaked into Ogallala with

some wild cock-and-bull story about Thorpe's fixing to gun me. He gets this kid girl all stirred up with the idea that the only way to save us from all getting kilt is to get you and your gunmen to balance off Thorpe's gunmen. That's why Jody and me had a row—if you want to call it that, because I wouldn't take any stock in the cock-and-bull yarn, and wouldn't throw in with a bunch of criminals if I did. That's what she means in this here note, and that's why she went looking for you. And that's why God knows where she is tonight! By God, Roper, there's not a man in the West has more to answer for than—"

"If a man of mine says Thorpe has decided to rub you out, you most likely'll get rubbed out," Roper told him. "Quite a few of my boys have a knack of finding out such things."

"If you figure you can use a flimsy game like that to get a penny's worth of backing out of King-Gordon—"

"I wouldn't use your backing to rub on a horse as a cure for mange," Roper told him. "That's what I think of that. I sent no man anywhere near you nor your girl. Who was this feller claimed to be hooked up with me?"

"A little sniveler called Shoshone Wilce. Everybody knows he was a scout coyote for you, before Texas ever run you out."

"Nobody run me out of any place," Roper said, but his mind whipped to something else. It was true that he talked to certain men in the town before he had come here. Now suddenly, he knew that he had learned what he had come to find out. He buttoned his coat and pulled on his gloves.

Gordon confronted him stubbornly. “I mean you shan’t leave here without telling me what you know.”

A glint of hard amusement was plain in Bill Roper’s eyes. “I know what you’ve told me. But I’ll add this onto it. I think you’ll soon have your girl back. I’m walking out of here now, Lew, because it’s time for me to look into a couple of things. But I’ll be seeing you—if Thorpe don’t get you first.”

The veins stood out sharply on Lew Gordon’s forehead, highlighted by a faint dampness. “In all fairness, I’ll tell you this,” he said. “It’s true I can’t lift a gun on you, or on any man who stands with empty hands. But as soon as you’re out of that door, all Miles City will be on the jump to see you don’t get loose. Twenty thousand hangs over your head, my boy!”

“Quite a tidy little nest egg,” Roper agreed. “I’d like to have it myself.”

A trick of the wind sent a great whirl of papers across the room as he went out.

He had not come here without providing that the horse which waited under his saddle was fresh and good. He struck westward now out of Miles City, unhurrying. At the half mile, he found a broad cross trail where some random band of cattle had trampled the snow into a trackless pavement. He turned north in this, followed it for a mile, then swung northwest over unmarked snow. Now that this horse was warmed a little, he settled deep in his saddle and pushed the animal into a steady trot. At that gait, even in the snow, he could expect the tough range-bred pony to last most of the night.

CHAPTER TWENTY-FOUR

A tired horse is not much inclined to shy, toward the end of a long day's travel, and when Bill Roper's horse snorted and jumped sidewise out of its tracks, the rider looked twice, curiously, at the carcass which had spooked his pony. A dead pony on the winter range being a fairly common thing, he was about to ride on when he noticed something about this particular dead pony that caused him to pull up and dismount for a closer examination.

After leaving Lew Gordon, he had ridden deep into the night, and though his pony had proved disappointing, he had made fast enough time so that now, an hour and a half before sunset, he was in the low hills which hemmed the valley of the Fork. Half an hour would bring him within sight of the Fork Creek rendezvous, and he was eager to push on, so that his deduction as to Jody's whereabouts might have a quick answer, one way or the other. But when he had examined the dead pony, he was glad that he had checked.

This was no winter-killed pony. The bright trace of frozen blood that had first caught Roper's eye was the result of two gunshot wounds in neck and quarters. The pony had been well fed and bore the saddle marks of recent hard riding. Evidently, it had wandered some distance since its rider had pulled off the saddle and turned it loose to shift as it could.

A dark foreboding possessed Roper as he studied the dead pony. Roper himself was short-cutting through the hills, following no trail. The coincidence that he had stumbled upon the carcass in all those snowy wastes could be accounted for only in one way: both Roper and the pony had followed a line of least resistance through the hills—a line that had the Fork Creek rendezvous at its far end. His discovery told him that there had been fighting at Fork Creek within the last forty-eight hours. If he was right in believing that Jody had come to Fork Creek—

He remounted and swung northward, mercilessly whipping up his weary pony, but approaching the Fork Creek camp roundabout, behind masking hills and through hidden ravines. An hour passed before he threw down his reins and crept on hands and knees to the crest of a ridge commanding the valley of the Fork.

The soft snow of two days before had at first begun to melt but was now frozen hard under the lash of a bitter wind. The steely glaze of its crust caught the sunset with strange red reflections, filling the valley with an unnatural light. Peering through an ice-hung bit of wolfberry bush, Roper made out, far up the valley, an irregularity in the snow that was the Fork Creek rendezvous.

For a little while, he could not be sure whether or not smoke rose from the camp. If anyone was here, they were being mighty careful what kind of fuel they burned. He decided at last that a faint haze hung over the brush where the cabin stood. His blood stirred, making a tingle in his cold hands.

He moved a half mile closer and resumed his watch, but for some time, he could make out nothing more.

Then, just as the sun set, three men moved out of the cabin. For a moment or two, they stood in the snow close together. One went back into the cabin. The two others disappeared for a moment, to reappear mounted. They separated, and Roper watched them ride in opposite directions up the nearest slopes of the hills. These passed beyond his sight, but in another minute or two their ways were retraced by two other riders.

"Outposts," Roper decided. "Somebody's keeping a hell of a careful watch."

The light was failing now. Roper was about to leave his lookout when something else happened that held him fastened to the ground.

To his right, surprisingly close, a rifle spoke, once only. Roper could neither see the man who had fired nor guess his target. He waited five minutes, gun ready, then stood up and moved his pony downslope into a shallow draw in which it was hidden by the brush. Moving cautiously, he proceeded north along the cut, seeking the position of the man who had fired.

Through the hillside brush a figure moved, crouching so low that his dark shape resembled a bear. After a moment, Bill Roper was able to make out that the approaching man carried a light carbine, and instead of cowboy boots, he wore the heavy shoe packs of some of the northern Indian tribes. A beaked cap was tied down on his head by a heavy muffler so that Roper could not see his face.

The man with the carbine moved swiftly down the hillside, sliding on the hard crust of the snow, but surprisingly silent in the brush.

"Indian, or half-breed," Roper thought, "a scout for whoever holds the cabin. Maybe getting in a little meat hunting as he goes."

The watched man dropped into the ravine, angling toward the bend where Roper stood. Bill Roper pulled himself out of the gully. He was crouched in dense brush, gun in hand, as the scout appeared below him.

Roper stood up. "Steady," he said.

The man in the draw jumped as if he had been struck, but as he raised his hands, he straightened so that Roper saw his face.

"Damn my soul!"

His captive was Shoshone Wilce.

"By God," said Shoshone, "I was never so glad to see anybody in my life!"

Roper's voice bit like frosty ice. "You know where she is?"

"Yeah," said Shoshone. "Yeah, I know where she is."

Roper dropped into the gully to snarl close into Shoshone's face. "Is she alive? Is she all right?"

"Oh, yeah, sure," Wilce assured him. "She's alive, all right. Don't seem like she's hurt any. I—"

"Don't seem like?" Roper repeated. "Damn your hide, where is she?"

"Bill, seems like them bastards have her down there at that cabin, and won't leave her loose."

"Who won't?"

"Bill, I don't know who."

"Well, how the devil did she get there?"

"Me," Shoshone said. He met Roper's eye bleakly. Obviously, he knew that he was in trouble here. "I brought her."

"What in all hell—"

"She would have come anyway, Bill. She was dead set on locating you. She didn't have nobody else to ride with her. I figured you'd sooner I'd try to bring her direct to you, so somebody would be with her, than have her wandering loose around the country by herself. A bartender in Miles told me you were here, and we rode here. And then—and then—"

"Well, then—what?"

"As I come into the valley," Shoshone said,

"seemed to me like something was wrong. But I couldn't make out what. We come up to the cabin careful and slow in the dark. But they seen us coming and they laid for us, I guess. Before we knew what had busted, they gunned her pony down, and they drilled mine twice so bad that I had to turn him loose. Most likely he's dead by now. I—" Shoshone hesitated.

"And you run out and left her," Bill filled in for him.

"Bill, I swear, I wouldn't have done nothing like that, not for no amount. Thing was, they was all around me. I couldn't see where to shoot or who they was. I figured first it was your own boys, making a mistake, and after I seen it wasn't, I just figured to keep in a fighting position, you might say, and close in first chance. Only—"

"Only you never saw any chance," Roper said with contempt.

"Well, no. There's seven of 'em down there, Bill, and they keep an awful steady watch. After I seen my horse was through, I tried to catch me another but couldn't make out. So I cut up my saddle blanket and chaps and made these here shoe packs, like the tribes do, so I could get around without leaving so much trail. And I been scouting 'em steady ever since. Sometimes I get in a long shot at one or another of 'em. This carbine don't carry so very good, but I plugged two of 'em; don't know how bad. And—"

"How the hell do you know she wasn't shot or hurt when her horse went down?" Roper demanded. "By God, Shoshone, if you let anything happen to that girl—"

"They let her walk outside sometimes during the day," Shoshone said. "That's how I seen she's all right."

"Can you make out who the bunch down there is?"

"I figure they're some Thorpe gun squad, out after your scalp. I figure they was laying to gun you. And now that they got the girl, I figure that they aim to hold her for bait, kind of."

"You figure! But you don't know?"

"Fact is, Bill, I don't know, not for sure."

Shoshone fell silent, and Roper, deep in thought, let him rest.

"You're most likely right," Roper said morosely at last. "There's four or five of these Thorpe war parties out after me, and this could easily be one. But of all the infernal luck I ever saw—What did Jody want with me? Did she tell you?"

"Thorpe has made up his mind to kill her old man," Shoshone said. "I went and told her, because I thought you'd want her to know, so she could maybe look out for him some. But the old man wouldn't listen to her, and they had a row. So then the only thing she could think of was to come to you. She's got some notion of trying to get you and her old man together again."

"Hell of a fine chance!"

"That's what I told her. But she—"

"Why in God's name," Roper flared at him again, "didn't you go after help?"

"I figured I'd get strung up for sure," Shoshone said flatly, "if I went and told Gordon what I'd done. I wanted to come for you, but naturally I didn't know where you'd went. The only thing I could figure out, I better try to ghost around these hills and maybe whittle 'em down to my size."

Roper snorted.

"How many boys you got with you?" Shoshone asked.

"Not one," Roper answered. "I was clear over on the Little Dry when Hat Crick Tommy brought word the girl had disappeared. I didn't figure, then, it was a fighting job. After I got to Miles, I went and talked to Gordon—"

"You talked to Gordon? How in hell—"

"I just walked in and talked to him," Roper said with irritation. "After Gordon convinced me that Jody had left Miles with you, I had a good idea where to come. I'd already talked to the bartender who sent you here. But then it was too late to go back after any of my riders, scattered out like they were."

"If only some of the Gordon cowboys would show up—"

"No chance of that. Gordon knows that the girl was looking for me. This made a good camp for me because it's a Lasham line camp—right in the heart of his northern range. Lasham never suspected I'd have the guts to use it, until now, and it sure would never come into Gordon's mind."

"Couldn't you have told Gordon—"

"I tell you, I never thought there'd be any fighting in this, until I found your dead pony."

"Bill," said Shoshone slowly, "this is terrible bad."

Just how bad it was and what it meant. Bill Roper could not decide. He was remembering now what Lew Gordon had said, "You've started things no mortal man can stop . . ."

"You say there are seven men in the cabin," Roper asked at last, "and two wounded?"

Shoshone nodded. "They ain't all in the cabin all of the time. Seems like they must have had the girl tell 'em that she come here to meet you. Naturally, they'd think you knew she was coming. Most likely they figure that if I ain't dead I'm carrying you word that will bring you here a-kiting. So they're holding her there now until they see if they can't get you. I ain't watched those fellers for fifteen years without knowing how they work."

"They're taking an awful chance," Roper said, iron death in his eye. "If I rode in here, warned, with my wild bunch—"

"It ain't such a bad chance they're taking,"

Shoshone contradicted. “Night and day their outposts are out. Two men can check the whole country daytimes, so they can see you coming twenty miles. You only got here because you come up through the timber to the south, on the trail from Miles—the last way they’d figure you’d come. Nights, there are more men on look-out than that, near as I can make out, and their lookout is strongest just before dawn—I suppose Iron Dog taught ’em that trick in the old days, always striking just before daylight, and now they can’t get it out of their heads. Night and day, they got ponies saddled. If ever they spotted your wild bunch riding in, they’d be almighty hard to catch.”

“If only,” Roper said, “the wild bunch was going to ride in! But it isn’t.”

“Maybe there’s some way we could fake it, so they’d give up and clear out. I figure they’d leave the girl behind if ever they set out to run.”

Roper shook his head. “No way to do that, Shoshone. By God, if those coyotes don’t hang for this—”

“How can they ever hang? If they’re Thorpe men, they got the law back of ’em. The girl rides in of her own accord, and something happens to her horse. They don’t give her a new horse for fear she’ll lose herself. There’s nothing in that that calls for an hour in jail for one of ’em, Bill.”

"Some of 'em aren't going to live to see a jail," Roper promised himself.

"What you going to do?"

"I'm going down and smoke 'em out. I'm going to smoke 'em out before the sun ever comes up again, and you're going to help me."

Shoshone nodded. "If we tackled 'em just before daylight, when the outpost is strong, and the cabin is weak—"

They talked it over for a long time. In the hidden gulch where Shoshone had been holing up, they made coffee and cooked meat and completed their plans.

"We can get in," was Shoshone's verdict at last. "We can get in, and we can take the cabin. But God knows how we're ever going to get out."

"I've got a plan for that," Roper said.

He wouldn't tell Shoshone what it was.

CHAPTER TWENTY-FIVE

There were no stars when Roper roused himself in his blankets, and he had no mechanical means of telling the time. Yet he knew very definitely that dawn was just two hours away. Raised on the Trail, he had learned by the changing of a thousand night guards to estimate the hour of the night with an accuracy which he no longer questioned.

He shook Shoshone Wilce. The little man groaned once, then came full awake with the sudden response of an animal.

"Time to go, Shoshone."

"I'm ready, Bill."

Without the snow, the rock-like impenetrability of the overcast sky would have made the night utterly black, but the ghostly pallor of the snow had the effect of faintly modifying the darkness. The eye might possibly have made out a moving dark shape at ten yards. Beyond that, there was nothing but a muffling blackness.

"You lead out," Roper said. His voice was instinctively hushed, even at this distance from the enemy. "You've had more chance to study the lay than me."

Shoshone Wilce delayed. "Bill," he said, "I lay thinking about this thing for a long time, after you was asleep." A dogged stubbornness came into his tone. "I figure we can probably take the cabin. And if we take the cabin without fighting, we've got a chance to get away. But if so much as one shot is fired—Bill, the outposts will close like a b'ar trap. I don't see no way we can ever get clear."

By the sudden frozen silence, Shoshone Wilce was able to sense Bill Roper's anger.

"I wish to God," Bill Roper said at last, "I had Hat Crick Tommy here, or Tex Long, or even the very greenest kid cowboy that's riding the range with them somewhere tonight. I need one other man for this job. It wouldn't take an especially brave man, or smart man, nor a real good gun-fighter. I just need one fairly good man. But I haven't even got that!"

"Bill, I only claim—look, Bill, I ain't afraid of 'em. I only—"

"You ain't afraid," Bill Roper repeated, "no—not much. But when the guns spoke, you left a girl down under her horse in the snow—maybe hurt, maybe dead—and you ran for your life."

When Bill Roper had said that, both were utterly still, while a man might have counted a hundred.

Shoshone's voice was flat and dead. "Is that the way it looks to you?"

"Look at it yourself."

“Then,” Shoshone said, “I guess there ain’t anything more to say.” He stood up.

“There’s this to say,” Bill Roper said. “You’re going to work with me tonight because I haven’t got anybody else. You’re going to do exactly what I say, and when I say, without any back talk or question. You make one slip tonight, and the West won’t hold you, nor the world won’t hold you, and you’ll answer to me in the end. You hear me?”

“Okay,” Shoshone said in the same flat, dead voice.

“One thing more,” Roper said. “If we make a quiet job, we’ll try to go out slow and quiet, the three of us together. Otherwise, you take Jody’s lead rope and ride like hell. Six miles below here, near the creek, there’s a kind of a brush corral. You and the girl will wait for me there. Wait for me until daylight begins to come; then go on.”

“Okay.”

“Lead out.”

They moved down into the valley of the Fork, walking fast. Shoshone carried his carbine in the crook of his arm, but Roper’s rifle was behind in his saddle boot. He had relied principally upon his six-gun for a long time. Roper had cut up a blanket and bound his boots with the strips, to avoid the creak and crunch of heels upon the frozen snow. The two men made little sound.

When they had dropped into the bed of Fork

Creek itself, they moved northward, following its windings, for what seemed a long way. But no sign of approaching dawn yet showed, and Roper felt that they had plenty of time. As they at last passed the point where the cabin stood, invisible in the dark, Shoshone indicated its location with raised arm, but they moved on fifty yards farther, so that they might approach the cabin from the north.

Cautiously now, Shoshone climbed the bank, silent as the Indians with whom he had spent his youth. Turning, he gripped Bill Roper's arm. Mis words were whispered close to Roper's ear.

"One of the night guards is out that-a-way, about five hundred yards," he whispered, "about in line with where you see that big dead pine."

Roper could see no dead pine, good as his eyes were. It annoyed him that Shoshone's eyes were better than his own—as good as the eyes of an Indian, or a lynx.

"I'll leave my carbine standing just outside the door," Shoshone said. "I only want it for later, after we've took to the horses."

"That's all right," Roper said. "But you remember this: If there's any trouble in the cabin, by God, you stand and fight! Because if you don't, I'll turn and plug you myself, if it takes my last shot to do it."

"Okay."

Roper went ahead now, walking boldly across

the snow. Better, he thought, to simulate the casual approach of friends than to depend upon a hope of complete surprise.

As he raised his hand to the door, a strange thrill of dread momentarily stirred him at the thought that Jody Gordon was inside—with whom? He glanced at Shoshone to make sure that the man was at his elbow. Then, his gun out, he flung wide the door. The slab door resisted, wedged in the ice of the sill, then shuddered open with a noisy violence.

Roper stepped in with a sidewise step that at once made room for Shoshone and brought Roper within the wall, clear of a possible shot from behind him in the dark.

"Don't anybody move!"

The uncertain and flickering light of the little fire seemed to fill the room with ample light, compared to the heavy darkness without. A man who sat upon a keg by the fire sprang up, his clawed hand reaching out to a gunbelt that lay upon the crude table, but the reaching hand rose empty in a continuous motion as the man put up his hand. Three crude bunks ranged along the rear wall. From the first of these, the one nearest the fire, a man came out with his hands up. One of his arms was heavily bandaged, and its upward motion carried its sling with it.

Now, Shoshone, whose heel had kicked the door shut behind him as he came in, made a headlong dive into the second of the three bunks. In that instant, the thing happened that Roper most dreaded, so that in a single split fraction of a second their chances were irrevocably hurt.

As Shoshone Wilce sprang, a gun smashed out from within the shadowy bunk. The blast of its explosion was magnified in the close quarters, leaving the ears ringing in the instant of stunned silence that followed.

The barrel of Shoshone's .45 had crashed upon the skull of the man in the bunk almost in the same instant that the shot was fired. A lean hand, gripping a six-gun, dropped out over the side of the bunk, relaxed slowly, and the six-gun slid to the floor from long, dangling fingers. Shoshone Wilce held absolutely motionless for a moment, half crouched, then straightened slowly.

"Shoshone—you hit?"

"It's only—" Shoshone began. His face was ghastly, and his voice quavered, but when he had fully straightened, it steadied again into the same dead flatness as before. "It's only—a kind of scratch along the ribs. I'm all right."

"Jody! Jody, is it you?"

Jody Gordon had been curled up in the corner of deepest shadows. She stood up now, white-faced, her movements uncertain. Then suddenly, the firelight caught the glint of the instant tears that overbrimmed her eyes.

"Bill! I thought they'd kill you!" She flung her

arms about his neck with the swift impulse of a child and kissed his mouth.

The man nearest the table made a sidelong movement toward the holstered gun that lay there. Bill Roper smashed a shot into the wall beside him, and the man jerked backward.

"Shoshone, can you ride?"

There was a curious strain in the flatness of Shoshone's voice. "I'm okay, I tell you."

Bill Roper caught up a sheepskin coat with his free hand and flung it over Jody's shoulders. "Get gone!" he snapped. "Shoot free the ponies' tie-ropes, and ride like hell! Here—take this!" He thrust the gunbelt from the table into Jody's unready hands. "I'll see you—where I said."

"Bill," said Shoshone, "if it's the same to you, I'd rather hold them here while you ride with her."

"Get gone, I said! You—"

"Bill, I tell you, I—"

Bill Roper bellowed at him, "You want to die?"

"Okay," Shoshone said, in that same strained, lifeless tone. He seized Jody's wrist, tore open the door with the hand that still held his gun, and was gone into the dark.

When they were gone, Bill Roper stood listening. Outside, two shots rang, a moment apart, as Shoshone shot the tied ponies free. Then sounded a swift crackle of the ice crust under their hoofs as two horses galloped down-valley, and Roper knew that Shoshone and Jody Gordon were on their way.

Bill Roper estimated that he had a few seconds left. Unhurriedly, almost leisurely, he picked up the gun dropped by the man in the bunk and thrust it in his own belt. After that, he collected three or four other weapons in a brief search that seemed perfunctory, yet it was effective because of his own practiced knowledge of where a range rider is apt to put his gun. These he kicked into a little heap beside the door, so that he would know where they were.

The man with the wounded arm spoke thickly. "You'll never get out of here alive," he told Roper.

"I wouldn't worry about that, was I you," Roper said. He slammed another harmless shot over the speaker's head, interestingly close to the man's scalp. He needed a continued sound of action at the cabin to draw the outposts in, so that Shoshone and Jody Gordon would have their chance to get clear.

After that, a full minute passed and stretched to a minute and a half. Evidently, the outposts had been farther away from the cabin than Shoshone had calculated, but Roper heard none of them fire.

He thought, "If I can keep them interested just ten minutes more—"

Now, a furiously ridden horse was coming up.

Roper flattened himself against the wall beside the open door and waited until he heard the man drop from his pony just outside. He stepped to the door, fired once, and a man crashed face downward upon the door sill itself to lie utterly motionless.

With his boot, Roper pushed the inert heap off the door sill, so that the door might be closed at need. Because there were only two more shots in his gun, he picked up one of the weapons he had collected and checked its loading.

"I'd stand real still if I was you," he warned the two who stood with their hands up. He fired one more shot between them, for purposes of general discipline. "I ought to kill you. Maybe I will in a minute—haven't decided yet."

Now, another horse was coming in fast. In another second or two, it would string into view around the corner of the cabin.

Roper cast a quick glance to see that his captives were where he thought they were. They had not moved. He dropped to one knee beside the door and fired twice quickly as a shape, dark on darkness, whirled around the corner of the cabin.

That was all—the end of the one-man war he had started to cover the retreat of Shoshone. He never remembered the shock of the blow that downed him. All consciousness ended at once, as sharply as if cut off with a knife.

He never knew which of the two men behind him sprang forward to smash him down, but he knew as soon as he knew anything at all that a long time had passed—more time than he could afford to lose.

CHAPTER TWENTY-SIX

Nobody but an old range rider could have located in the dark the brush corral where Shoshone Wilce and Jody Gordon were supposed to wait for Bill Roper. What would have been a simple problem by daylight, in darkness became a test of scouting ability and cowman's instinct. Yet somehow, by the throw of the land, and by his deep knowledge of the habits of thought of cowmen, Shoshone Wilce nosed out that circular corral of brush, in a darkness so thick that he was uncertain he had found the landmark until he had touched it with his hands.

A faint line of gray was already appearing on the rim of the world, and a whisky-jack was calling raucously somewhere in the scrub pine.

"It's almost daylight already," Jody Gordon said, fear in her voice. "If he doesn't come soon—if he doesn't come—"

She broke off, unable to go on. "Half an hour," Shoshone Wilce said. "We'll wait half an hour."

"And then—?"

"We've got to go on."

"I can't! Not if he doesn't come. We'll have to go back. We'll have to try—"

"He said go on. We have to do like he said." Shoshone's voice dropped to a curious, fierce whisper. "Whatever happens—you remember that! You have to go on!"

They waited then, while five minutes passed. Shoshone Wilce kept his pony moving slowly up and down to prevent its stiffening up by too rapid a cooling after its run, and Jody followed his example.

"Listen here," Shoshone Wilce said at last. He dropped his voice and sat motionless. For a moment or two, there was no sound there except the rhythmic breathing of the hard-run ponies. "I want to tell you something," Shoshone resumed, his voice low, husky, and strangely unsteady. "It looks like I run away and left you when your pony was shot down. I see now it looks like that. But I want you to know I didn't go to do nothing like that, Miss Gordon."

"I know," she said, "it was the only—"

"I shouldn't have done it," Shoshone said. "I wouldn't do it if I was doing it again. I figured I'd be more use to you if I could keep my horse on its feet. I figured I could best handle it like an Indian would—pick 'em off one at a time and make sure. But I'd do different if I had it to do again."

"What else could you have possibly done? There wasn't any chance for anything else."

"I should have stood and fought," Shoshone said. "Like he would have done."

"It was better this way," Jody told him. "Don't you worry about it, Shoshone."

Shoshone said vaguely, "I want you to tell him about it. I want you to tell him I'd do different if I had it to do again."

"Why don't you tell him yourself?"

"Maybe I will. But if anything comes up—so's I don't get the chance—"

"Of course I'll tell him."

They fell silent, and after that a long time passed. Shoshone stopped walking his horse and sat perfectly motionless close to the wall of the brush corral. The gray light increased, while they waited for what seemed an interminable time. It seemed to Jody that in a few minutes more they would have to admit that daylight was upon them, as it seemed to her that an hour, two hours, had passed, instead of the half hour which Shoshone had decided they could wait. But still, Bill Roper did not come.

"Do you suppose he could have ridden past?" Jody asked.

"No," Shoshone said, very low in his throat.

When she could stand the suspense no more, Jody Gordon dismounted. The inaction and the cold was stiffening her in the saddle, and now she led her pony while she stamped and swung her arms.

She thought, "I'll lead my pony five times around the outside of the corral. He'll be here by then . . . he must be here by then."

She wondered, as she slowly led her pony around the circle marked by the walls of brush, what she would do if Roper did not come—if he never came. Perhaps go on? Perhaps go back . . .

Jody Gordon was fighting back an overwhelming, impossible panic. She knew the cool, hard sufficiency of the men against whom Roper had pitted himself. From the standpoint of her father, who had turned against him, she knew the unassuageable bitterness, the vast sinister malevolence which Roper had raised against himself by the miracles of the Texas Rustlers' War. If he were caught now in the grip of that malevolence—

It took all her will power to restrain herself from breaking into a run, or from mounting her pony and racing him—where? Any place, if only her high-strung nerves could find expression in action. But she forced herself to lead her pony slowly, measuring her strides while the daylight increased.

Then, as she completed the circuit of the corral and came again to where Shoshone's pony stood, she saw that Shoshone Wilce no longer sat the saddle. At first, she thought that he had tied his pony and walked away, but as she came nearer, she saw that the little man was down in the snow, huddled against the rough brush of the corral barrier.

She sprang forward, calling out his name, and there was a meaningless, nightmarish quarter of a minute while her pony reared backward from the sudden jerk upon its bridle and had to be quieted before she could advance again.

"Shoshone! What's the matter? Are you—are you—?"

Shoshone's eyes were half-open. He was not asleep, but he did not answer. And now as she dropped to her knees beside him in the snow, she saw that a bright trickle of red had traced a line from the corner of his mouth, crookedly across his chin.

"Shoshone!"

In the ugly panic that swept her, it was many seconds before she could fully comprehend that Shoshone Wilce was dead.

CHAPTER TWENTY-SEVEN

"We're making a big mistake, not to hang him and be done with it," Red Kane said.

They were two days from Fork Creek now. This long and narrow room, which Jim Leathers paced so restlessly, was the kitchen of the main house at Walk Lasham's southwest camp—a convenient stopover on the way to Sundance, where Roper was to be turned over to Ben Thorpe.

Even though Walk Lasham himself was not here, this camp held a peculiar interest for Bill Roper. Since the day when Roper had taken the southward trail from Ogallala, at the beginning of his own long war, he had seen Walk Lasham only once. Yet that dark, long-faced man with the lean, stooped shoulders had been a figure very often in his mind. The great power of Ben Thorpe in the north was inseparable from Walk Lasham, who himself had built it. All through the northern raids, Lasham had remained a shadowy opposing force, so deeply entrenched as to seem unbeatable sometimes. It was interesting to Roper now to sit in this lonely cabin, which, ordinary though it might be, served as the headquarters of the man he had worked against for so long.

"The quicker we hang him, the better off we'll be," Red Kane said again.

Wearily, doggedly, Jim Leathers rolled a cigarette. He took his time about replying. "Seems like you already said that once before."

"I'm liable to keep on saying it," Red Kane told him. "Things is different now."

This camp had a separate bunkhouse for its heavy force of riders, but the cabin in which they sat, nevertheless, had a second room—a small storeroom which also contained three or four bunks. In its doorway, behind the two men who watched Bill Roper, a girl now appeared, a slim, full-breasted girl, whose dark, slanting eyes had sometimes troubled Bill Roper before now.

He had not been surprised to find Marquita here in Walk Lasham's southwest cow camp, to which his captors had brought him. He had guessed, when he had last talked to her in Miles City, that she was Walk Lasham's girl, and in spite of her expressed eagerness to leave Lasham and ride with Roper, he realized that Marquita still had to live in some way.

Girls of her stamp could not afford to throw down such a man as Lasham until more interesting opportunities offered.

Her face was impassive now, but one of the slanting dark eyes narrowed in a definite signal to Roper. The combination of Spanish and Indian blood in this girl from the Texas border gave her a lithe, lazy grace, and a haunting depth in her dark eyes, and that same blood made her unaccountable—sometimes stoic and smoldering, sometimes livened by the lightning flashes of an inner fire. Undoubtedly, she was capable of a passionate devotion and an equally passionate cruelty. Anything could happen in a situation that included Marquita—with Marquita in love.

For a moment, Bill Roper resented the fact that he couldn't be interested in any girl except Jody Gordon—a girl who didn't want him or need him. All the worst aspects of his own situation were apparent to him, then. He was an outlaw, wanted the length of the Trail, and probably would be an outlaw all the rest of his life, which gave every promise of being a short one. That even Marquita wanted him, or had any use for him, was a gift which he should have been glad to accept. What he had to think of now, though, was that Marquita was extremely likely to precipitate a lot of immediate disturbance.

Troubled, he wished to shake his head, or in some other way caution her that she must make no attempt to interfere. Roper had no intention of ever coming into the hands of Ben Thorpe alive. Somewhere between this place and Sundance, where Thorpe waited, he would make his play, however slim the chance. Yet he would rather take his chances with some unforeseen opportunity later, when they were again on the trail, than to be plunged into some helpfully intended situation which the girl might devise—with danger to herself and questionable advantage to him. She had never brought him any luck.

He was unable, however, with the eyes of his two enemies upon him, to signal her in any way.

"Ben wanted him alive, if I could get him," Jim Leathers said stubbornly. "Well, I got him alive, and I aim to keep him that way. You bums ain't going to talk me into anything different just because you figure a dead man is easier to pack."

Bill Roper listened sardonically. In the two days spent in traveling from the Fork Creek rendezvous, the scalp wound which had brought him down had nearly healed, but when he laced his fingers behind his head, he winced and dropped his hands again.

It was typical of the quality of his captors that his hands were not tied or manacled. They told him where to sit, and they made him stay put, and they were careful that no opportunity was given him to snatch a gun from an unwary holster, but these were merely the routine precautions of sensible men. For these riders were the picked gunfighters of Ben Thorpe's scores of outfits—and a lifetime spent in the handling of fighting outfits had enabled Thorpe to pick men who were the equal of any in the West. They did not fear Roper, would not have feared him had he been armed.

Bill Roper had no doubt that Red Kane and perhaps one or two of the others would kill a doomed prisoner for no more reason than Jim Leathers had suggested. He could see, though, that Red Kane was wasting his time. Jim Leathers was the type of man that nobody could bulldoze into anything. Having decided what he was going to do, the opposition of the others would only increase Leathers's stubbornness, making it impossible for him to change his mind even if he should decide he had been wrong.

"If only we'd found Walk Lasham here," Red Kane grumbled, "I'll bet, by golly—"

Jim Leathers shot a hard glance at Kane, and Roper knew that Red Kane had not helped his case with Leathers by bringing in Lasham's name. Probably Leathers would like to fill Lasham's shoes, if the truth was known.

"He'll be at Sundance with Ben Thorpe," Jim Leathers said drily. "You can talk to him then."

"And a fine time for it that will be," Red Kane argued, unable to abandon his point. "Here we got the chance of a lifetime to do something big. In place of taking just this one varmint in, we could just as soon go back with the scalps of the big end of 'em. Suppose instead of just bringing Roper in we come in with the scalps of Dry Camp Pierce—Hat Crick Tommy, Dave Shannon, Tex Long?"

Bill Roper could not resist taunting them with a loud snicker.

Red Kane wheeled on him. "What the hell's the matter with you?"

"Any one of those boys would eat you alive."

"You were supposed to be top dog of 'em all," Red pointed out. "And where are you?"

"Oh," Roper grinned, "you're hoping to get 'em from behind?"

Red Kane stared at him a moment like an angry steer, and then ignored him, his mind holding steadfastly to his argument.

"Here's this wild bunch playing right into our hands," he insisted to Leathers. "Last night—not four miles from here, by God!—they pick up five hundred head of Lasham's fattest stock. By morning, Bud and the Kid and the Lasham cowboys will have the lot of 'em cut off, no farther from here than the Big Coulee. The wild bunch are liable to be suckers enough to try to stand and fight a little bunch like that. We can get into it yet—and you and me, with the others—why, we can slam in there, and—"

The Lasham camp had been boiling with news as Jim Leathers's men had ridden in at dusk with their prisoner. Much had happened on the range while Leathers had waited out Bill Roper at the Fork Creek camp. The news that had reached Lasham's southwest camp was broken and seemed to have been little understood by the men who had brought it, but Roper, with his inside knowledge of the force he had turned loose against Lasham, could piece together its meaning well enough. Lasham's southwest outpost, with its big herds of picked cattle wintering in this deepest and richest of the Montana grass, had been more powerfully manned than any other Lasham camp. But twice in the past week, frantic calls for reinforcements from the outfits to the east had drained most of this manpower away—first five picked gun-fighters, then a dozen cowboys more, until only five men had been left.

The messengers who had killed their ponies to come for help had brought the camp a fragmentary story which gave Roper the deepest satisfaction. In their tales of incredible losses, of raiders who struck night after night at far separated points, driving cattle unheard-of distances to disappear weirdly in the northern wastes, Roper read the success of his Great Raid.

Dry Camp Pierce was sweeping westward across Montana like a destroying wind. By unexpected daring, by speed of movement, by wild riding relays which punished themselves no less than the cattle they drove, Dry Camp was feeding an increasing stream of Lasham beef into the hands of Iron Dog's bands, who spirited the beef forever from the face of Montana. By the very boldness of its conception and the wild savagery of its execution, the unbelievable Great Raid was meeting with success.

From his long experience, he could picture every pony-punishing ride of the raiders, could see every long mile of the vast terrain they harried. He could see the weather-wizened little Dry Camp Pierce, cow-thief extraordinaire, now leading the way in the masterpiece of all his outlaw career. He could see the youngster cowboys, turning gaunt and haggard-eyed in the relentless saddle grind, and he could see the long, heavy trampling lines of relayed cattle, heads down and quarters tucked under them, humping along at a swinging half-trot through cold dawns and dusks. Those things made a picture somehow somber in the immensity of its angry effort and the unparalleled damage of its effect. Yet, by the breadth of its audacity and the great sweep of its daring, it was touched with a red glory.

And now Dry Camp had struck even deeper than Roper had planned, lifting the best of Lasham's beeves from almost within gunshot of Lasham's strongest camp. So well had Dry Camp planned, and so steadily did the luck hold, that a full day had passed before the loss inflicted by the raiders was discovered. The five remaining cowboys at the southwest camp were only tightening their cinches as Jim Leathers rode in.

Most of the Leathers party had joined the Lasham men in pursuit of Dry Camp's raiders. Only Jim Leathers himself and the unwilling Red

Kane remained to convoy Roper to Ben Thorpe at Sundance.

Because of the confusion involved in the organization of the pursuit, the night was now far gone. Already, it was long past midnight.

"There's still another reason," Red Kane said, "why it would be a hell of a sight better to hang him now. Suppose that wild bunch of his knows he's here?"

"How the devil would they know that?" Leathers said with disgust.

"Maybe they was scouting us with spy glasses as we come over the trail today."

"If they was, they would have landed on us right then, in place of waiting till we got into camp."

"Maybe the girl run to them—"

"Hell! The girl! You make me sick."

"Have it your own way."

"You're damned right I'll have it my own way. I don't want to hear no more about it. And I'll tell you this: If your trigger finger gets itchy while you're on watch tonight, you better soak it in a pan of water, and leave the gun be. Because if anything comes up while you're on watch such that you got to shoot him, by God, next thing you got to shoot me—you understand?"

"I guess it could be done," Red Kane said nastily.

"Hold your horses, will you? You'll see him

hung quick enough. Now get out of here and get some sleep. I'm taking the first watch myself."

Red Kane hesitated. With the night already well turned toward morning, he should have been tired, but he was not. He turned a heavy gaze upon Marquita, obviously calculating. It was apparent to Roper that Kane was speculating how best to get Marquita into his own bunk without clashing with Jim Leathers again. Apparently, he arrived at a conclusion satisfactory to himself, because after a moment, he rose and shouldered out the door. Immediately, he stuck his head back in. "You better keep both lamps going. The little varmint is liable to try to kick out the light."

Leathers ignored this, and Red Kane disappeared. This time, the door shut after him.

Leathers said, "Get me a drink."

Marquita unhurriedly set out a bottle and a glass on the table beside Jim Leathers's elbow.

"A deck of cards," Leathers said.

Marquita produced this, too. As Leathers began to lay out a game of solitaire, Marquita moved idly toward one of the two kerosene lamps. Roper, watching her passively, saw that it was the lamp farthest from him; probably, if it went out, he could knock over the other by throwing his hat.

"Get away from that lamp," Leathers said.

Marquita strolled over to Leathers, the high heels of her slippers clicking lazily on the puncheon floor. "Why are you so cross with me?" she asked reproachfully. She moved behind Jim Leathers and slowly ran her fingers through his hair.

"Ain't going to get you a thing," Jim Leathers said sourly.

"No?" said Marquita. For a moment, one hand was lost in the folds of her skirt. Then deftly, unhurriedly, she planted the muzzle of a .38 against the back of Jim Leathers's neck.

CHAPTER TWENTY-EIGHT

There was a moment of absolute silence, absolute immobility. Jim Leathers's eyes were perfectly still upon Bill Roper's face, as still as his hands, in one of which a playing card hung suspended. But though his face did not notably change, Marquita, with her .38 pressed hard against the back of the gunman's neck, had turned white; her mouth worked as she tried to speak, and her wide eyes were upon Bill Roper in terrified appeal. Perhaps no more than a second could have passed in that way, but to them all it seemed as if time had stopped, so that that little fraction of eternity held them motionless forever.

Bill Roper, moving up and forward, exploded into action smoothly, like a cat. It was the length of the room between them that saved Jim Leathers then.

Leathers twisted, lightning fast, and Marquita's gun blazed into the floor as her wrist swept down in the grip of Leathers's left hand. And Bill Roper checked a yard from the table as Leathers's gun flashed into sight, becoming instantly steady. Marquita sagged away from Leathers, and her gun clattered upon the puncheons, but although Leathers's whole attention was concentrated upon Roper, Marquita's wrist remained locked in his grasp.

The gunfighter's voice was harder and colder than the steel of his gun, as hard and cold as his eyes.

"Get back there where you was."

Bill Roper shrugged and moved back.

Leathers flung Marquita away from him and, with his left hand, picked up her gun as the door of the storeroom was torn open and Red Kane bulged in.

"What the hell—"

"This bitch come behind me and stuck a gun in my neck," Leathers told him.

"The devil! You hurt?"

"Hell, no! I took it away from her."

Gently, tentatively, his long fingers ran over his wounded leg. That bullet wound in his thigh must have tortured him unspeakably through the two days in the saddle, and it must have been jerking at his nerves now with red-hot hooks, roused by the swift action that had preserved his command.

His face had turned gray so that the black circles under his eyes made them seem to burn from death's-head hollows, and his face, which had changed so little in this moment of action, was relaxed into an ugly contortion. Slowly, the gray color was turning to the purple of a dark and terrible anger.

"By God," said Red Kane, "I told you we should have hung him!"

"You told me right," Jim Leathers said. The

burn of his eyes never for a moment left Bill Roper's face. "You was right and I was wrong. I should have hung him at the start."

A pleasurable hope came into Red Kane's face. "Well—it ain't too late!"

"No, it ain't too late. Tie his hands."

Joyfully, Red Kane caught up a reata. "What you going to do? You going to—"

"I want to know if he whistles when the wind blows through him. I aim to hang him high enough so's I can find out." Then, to Marquita, who had tried to sidle out the dark door, "You get back here! I'd shoot you just as quick as him."

Keeping Roper between himself and Leathers, so that his partner's gun bore steadily upon Roper's belt buckle, Kane lashed Roper's hands behind him. The frost-stiff rope bit deep.

"Tie up this slut, too," Leathers ordered when Kane had finished. "I want her to see this show."

Marquita said, "I'm sorry, Bill." Her voice was broken by hard, jerking sobs, and tears were running down her face, yet somehow her words sounded dull and dead. "I did the best I could."

Roper was curiously moved. Part of his mind was telling him that, however loose the schedule of fidelity in Marquita's life might have been, she would gladly have died for Bill Roper now.

"You did fine," Roper said. "That was a game try."

“Move him out,” said Leathers, holstering his gun.

Hobbling on his stiff leg, Leathers moved to the outer door, flung it open, and, coatless, he stepped out into the bitter sweep of the wind. Then, abruptly, he stopped and signaled Red Kane back with one hand.

“Red, get back! Get out of line!”

With the quick instinct of a man who has always been in trouble, Red Kane jumped back into the room, carrying Bill Roper with him. They all could hear now the sound of running horses.

Jim Leathers, in spite of his warning to Kane, made no effort to move out of the light. Standing square in the door, he drew his gun. A bullet splintered into the casing beside him as the report of a carbine sounded from somewhere beyond. Jim Leathers fired twice, then stepped inside, closed, and barred the heavy door.

For a moment, the eyes of Kane and Leathers questioned each other.

“Dry Camp Pierce,” Kane said.

“Naturally.”

“If it don’t beat hell that they should land in at just this minute—”

“That’s no accident, you fool. Their Indian fighting way of doing business is they lay out on the hill, and slam down just before daylight. By God, they must have been watchin’ this dump all night!”

Red Kane said stupidly, “This ain’t daylight, this ain’t—”

“They heard the shot when she tried to gun me, I guess.” Leathers was very cool and quiet now. Deliberately, he pulled on his sheepskin. “Get out the back, untie the ponies, and get your man aboard.”

“Jim, seems like we stand a better chance here, way we are, than running in the open, what with—”

“They’ll burn us out if we try to hold. Get going, you!”

Dragging Roper after him, Kane plunged into the dark of the back room. He swore as he rummaged for his rifle, his sheepskin.

Leathers neither swore nor hurried. Moving deliberately, he blew out one lamp, hobbled across the room to the other. Then all hell broke loose at once.

The single frosted pane of the ten-inch window at the end of the room smashed out with a brittle ring of falling glass. In the black aperture appeared the face of a boy, pale and wild-eyed, so young-looking that he might almost have been called a child. The heavy .44 with which he had smashed the window thrust through the broken pane, and it blazed out heavily twice.

Jim Leathers, staggering backwards as if he had been hit with a log ram, fired once, from the level of his belt. The face vanished, but for a moment after it was gone, the hand that held the gun dangled limp within the room. Then the gun thudded on the floor, and the lifeless hand disappeared.

Jim Leathers reached for the wall and steadied himself for a moment. Then abruptly, he dropped to his knees, to all fours, and began to cough.

As Leathers went down, a broken roar of guns broke out in the storeroom. Leathers groped for his gun, tried to rise, but could not.

Roper, who had been dragged into the dark storeroom by Red Kane, felt the swift sting of the wind as the back door was smashed open, and was able to tear free as the guns began. He stumbled over piled sacks and flattened himself against the wall. The blind blasting in the dark of the back room lasted long enough for three guns to empty themselves. Their smashing voices fell silent with an odd suddenness, as suddenly as they had opened. In the dark, a voice said, "In God's name, let's have a light!"

After what seemed a long time, a match flared uncertainly, and Roper's quick glance estimated the changed situation. In the back room, now two men were down—Red Kane, and another whom Roper immediately recognized as an old King-Gordon cowboy called Old Joe.

The dim flicker of the match was augmented to a steady glow as a lantern was found and lighted. Roper did not recognize the other man in the room—the cowboy who had lighted the lantern with one hand, his smoking six-gun still ready in the other.

The stranger stooped over Old Joe. "You hurt bad?"

"It's only my laig, my laig."

The other stepped over the inert body of Kane to the door and surveyed the silent kitchen.

"Jim Leathers, by God! Somebody got Jim Leathers and got him hard!"

He stepped back into the rear room. "You're Bill Roper, aren't you? Where's the others?"

"There aren't any others. They all went out on Dry Camp's trail, after his raid day before yesterday."

"No others here? You sure?"

"Kane and Leathers are the only ones here."

Old Joe, both hands clasped on his smashed leg, spoke between set teeth. "Where's Jody? For God's sake, find Jody!"

The King-Gordon cowboy whom Roper did not know, went out, his spurs ringing with his long strides.

"Jody isn't here," Roper told Old Joe disgustedly. "She got loose two days ago."

"The hell she isn't here! She come here with us!"

"With you? But you're from Gordon's Red Butte camp, aren't you? I thought Jody went to Miles City with Shoshone Wilce."

"She never went to Miles. She knew Leathers was bringing you here, from what she'd heard him say. She come to us, because we was the K-G camp nearest here, and she wouldn't hear of nothin', but we come and try to crack you loose. Shoshone Wilce—he's daid."

Bill Roper was dazed. "I thought—I thought—"

The other cowboy now came tramping back into the cabin, an awkward burden in his arms, and this time, Jody Gordon herself followed close upon his heels. Her face was set, and the sharp flush across her cheekbones did not conceal her fatigue.

Bill Roper started to say, "Jody, how on earth—"

Jody did not seem to see him. She appeared to be thinking only of the slim youngster whom the cowboy carried. The cowboy laid the limp figure on the floor of the kitchen, ripped off his own neckerchief and spread it over the youngster's face.

Jody Gordon methodically shut the door. Then she dropped to the floor beside the fallen youngster, lifted his head into her lap, and gave way to a violent sobbing. The high-keyed nervous excitement that had sustained her through the hard necessities of action was unstrung abruptly, now that her work was done; it left nothing behind it but a great weariness, and the bleak consciousness that this boy was dead because of her.

Roper and the King-Gordon cowboy stood uncertainly for a moment. Then the cowboy picked up Leathers where he lay struggling for breath, carried him into the back room, and put him down on a bunk. For a moment, he hesitated, and then closed the door between the two rooms, leaving Jody alone.

"Seems like the kid got Jim Leathers, but Jim Leathers got the kid."

"Daid?" Old Joe asked.

"Deader'n hell! Jody's takin' it awful hard."

The cowboy cut loose Bill Roper's hands, and together they lifted Old Joe onto the other bunk. Roper cut Marquita free.

"Get me that kettle of water off the stove," Bill Roper ordered Marquita, and when she had brought it he said, "Now you go and keep Miss Gordon company for a little while."

Marquita left them, closing the door behind her.

Old Joe kept talking to them in a gaspy sort of way, as they did what they could for his wound.

"The kid was scared to death to come. Jody seen that and tried to send him back, with some trumped-up message or something. Naturally, he seen through that and wouldn't go. Now most likely she blames herself that he's daid. Lucky for us that Leathers's main outfit wasn't here."

"You mean just you three was going to jump the whole Leathers' outfit, and the Walk Lasham cowboys, too?"

“Not three—four,” Old Joe said. “Don’t ever figure that girl don’t pull her weight. We been laying up here on the hill since before dusk. She aimed we should use the same stunt you used at Fork Crick—bust into ’em just before daylight. Then somebody fires off a gun down here, and she loses her haid, and we come on down. It was her smashed her horse against the door, trying to bust it in. She blindfolded him with her coat—threw it over his haid—and poured on whip and spur, and she bangs into the planks. Broke his neck, most like. Cain’t see why she wasn’t killed—”

“Just you four,” Roper marveled, “were going to tackle the whole works, not even knowing how many were here?”

“We tried to tell her it couldn’t be done. But you can’t talk any sense into a woman, once she gets a notion in her nut.”

CHAPTER TWENTY-NINE

Marquita, closing the door of the storeroom behind her, for some moments stood looking down at Jody Gordon.

Jody still sat on the floor, upon her lap the head of the boy who had downed Jim Leathers. The sobs that convulsed her were dying off now, leaving her deeply fatigued and profoundly shaken.

"You might as well get up now," Marquita said. Her soft Mexican slur gave an odd turn to the blunt American words she used. "The fight's over, and that boy you've got there is dead as a herring. What you need is a drink."

Jody lifted her head, rubbing the tears from her eyes so that she could look at the other woman.

"Where's Billy Roper?" Jody demanded. "Is Billy all right?"

"Sure, he's okay. That other old cocklebur of yours got a slug in the leg. But Jim Leathers will most likely pull through, too, so that makes the score a tie."

"But—all the Leathers men—all the Lasham cowhands—where are they?"

"They all went out chasing after Dry Camp's raiders. Leathers and Red Kane were the only ones here—and your boys got Red Kane, and wounded Leathers."

With a visible effort, Jody Gordon pulled herself together and gently lowered the head of the dead boy to the floor. She got up shakily and, for a moment, looked at Marquita.

"I've seen you somewhere," Jody said. "Yes, I remember now. You worked in a dance hall in Uvalde."

"I don't know how you know that," Marquita said. Her voice was low and soft, without resentment. "You weren't ever in it."

"Everyone knows who everyone else is in Uvalde."

"That's true," Marquita said. "And so, of course, I know you are Jody Gordon, of the great King-Gordon. And you never worked in a dance hall, because you never needed to work."

Jody Gordon walked to the table and sat down. She leaned her elbows upon the plain boards and buried her face in her hands.

"It's my fault that boy is dead," Jody said brokenly. "He didn't want to come. None of them wanted to come. But this boy was afraid—afraid of the very name of Jim Leathers. And when I tried to send him back, he wouldn't go! And now he's lying here . . . he's lying here because of me."

"He died very well," Marquita said. "He got Jim Leathers—a good job of work for any man."

Jody did not answer. Marquita sat down opposite her and, for a little while, studied Jody.

"Why did you come here?" Marquita asked at last. Her voice continued gently curious—nothing more.

"I knew Billy Roper was alive," Jody told her. "Because I was watching when Leathers left Fork Creek with him. I already knew they meant to take him to Ben Thorpe at Sundance for the reward. That would be death, to him. And I knew they meant to stop over here on the way. So I got the boys from our Red Butte camp, and I come on . . ."

"You are a very foolish little girl," Marquita said. "Luck saved you, but if this camp had been full of men, it would have been suicide."

"Wouldn't you have done the same?"

Marquita shrugged impatiently, as if this was beside the point. "I feel very sorry for you," she said.

"Why?"

"Because I think you are in love with this Billy Roper."

"Why do you say that?"

"*Es claro*," Marquita said. "It is plain. And it's a pity, because this kind of man is not for you."

At first, Jody Gordon did not answer. But behind the softness of Marquita's voice was a cogency as strange as her American words—a cogency that would not be ignored. Here, Jody found herself facing a woman whom she could not possibly have understood. Marquita's careless, even reckless mode of life, her uncoded relationships with men—there was not an aspect of Marquita's life that did not deny every value of which Jody was aware. Marquita appeared to thrive and flower in a mode of life in which Jody incorrectly believed she herself would have died.

"I don't understand you."

Marquita's glance swept the room—the bare chinked walls, the dead boy. Her glance seemed to go beyond the door, where they were dressing Old Joe's wound, beyond the walls, to the cold windswept prairie, where men still rode this night, though morning was close.

"What do you know," she said—"what can you know of the lives of these men?"

Jody lifted her head then and looked at Marquita, and again, the simple words and the mask-like face of Marquita seemed to have a meaning for which she groped. In the silence that followed, it came to Jody that the night's fighting was not yet over, that she must still fight for herself and for Bill—and somehow for that foolish house in Ogallala, with its tall tower overlooking the plain.

"I was raised with Billy Roper," she said, stretching a point. But even as she said the words, she knew by Marquita's smile that this dance hall girl recognized the lie.

"Through all this time, where have you been?"

"You should know," Jody said with a flash of spirit. "My cowboys broke this thing wide open tonight!"

Jody felt the strange obsidian eyes stroke the whole length of her body, as if she were being undressed. "Your cowboys?" asked Marquita. "You mean your father's cowboys, no? Do you belong to one of these men, do one of these men belong to you?"

Marquita stood up, and, with the slow and deliberate stride that seemed a dramatization of her smile, she went to the window, and with one thumb tested a jag of the glass that the dead boy had struck out when he downed Jim Leathers. For a moment, her profile stood pale against that outer night which, moonless and starless, seemed to open into a world without direction, without any heart cuing or familiar landmark. Jody felt suddenly empty and lost.

"Do you ride with them?" the gentle, inexorable voice went on. "Do you share their blankets? Do you ride under their ponchos in the rain? Where are you when their guns speak? Who prays for them at dawn, knees down in this Godforsaken snow?"

Marquita paused, and her body swung, lazily assured, across a shadowy angle of the room toward the closed door that had hid Roper, working now over the wounded men. Her hands were spread against the doorposts, and it seemed to Jody, watching her, as if Marquita were a barrier between what might have been Jody's and that which she had lost now.

"You don't have to bar the door," she said.

Marquita's hands came away from the doorposts. "I know I don't."

The words were so indolently cadenced that they might have been spoken in Spanish. And at their soft assurance, something awoke in Jody Gordon . . . Something was still worth fighting for. Perhaps it had nothing to do with Bill Roper, but it flowed deep into the roots of her life, deeper than her life with one man—with any man—could ever flow. And as she looked at Marquita, strange things came to her that she herself could not have put into words.

Into her mind came the faces of Texas women, women with level, honest eyes and gnarled hands. Behind them were shadowy generations of other enduring women—all the westward pushing generations who had given so much of themselves to the land. Those women dared all things, faced all things, but somehow, always and immutably, they carried with them the traditions of a way of living.

When Jody Gordon thought of those women, she knew that Marquita and all her kind would presently pass. Perhaps Bill Roper, like all the rest of his bold riders, must also pass, but now, suddenly, Jody knew that whatever else might vanish from this prairie, what she herself stood for would remain. The hard riding and the savage raiding, the violent destruction and the violent pleasure—when those were gone, there would remain certain quiet things . . .

When she spoke at last, she scarcely recognized her own voice. It seemed to her that in the quiet her thoughts were going up those long dusty trails that had been King-Gordon's. And she was thinking forward, too, into a future where those trails would lead, even though Bill Roper would not be on them.

"I guess I was wrong," she said. Her words had a strange echo of Marquita's own directness. "You're Bill Roper's girl—is that what you wanted to tell me?"

The dance hall girl's words fell softly. "*Sí*, that is what I wanted you to know."

Jody stood up. She felt suddenly tired and numb.

"I still think a world can be made where decency can live," she said.

Beyond the splintered window, the wind blew bitter off the prairie, where there was yet no hint of light. But Jody's head was up, her eyes gray and clear. She seemed to speak through the smashed window frame to the dawn, which could not be far off.

"Leave us out of account," she said. "Someday,

decent things will live on this prairie, whatever happens to us. But meantime—I guess he belongs to you."

She held Marquita's stare for a moment, then turned and walked to the door. Opening it, she saw that the first forlorn cold gray of the winter dawn was coming into the sky east of Montana. The black hulk of the horse whose neck she had broken lay at her feet. She pulled from under it the coat with which she had blinded it when she charged the door and pulled it on; the bitter cold of the dawn was enough to penetrate to the bones.

Slowly, she uncinched and worked the saddle free, then the bridle. She staggered a little as she shouldered the saddle and walked out toward the corral where other, living ponies stood, dark humped-up shapes against the snow.

CHAPTER THIRTY

Bill Roper and Bob Stokes—The King-Gordon cowboy whom Roper had not known—had finished their makeshift dressing of Old Joe's wound and were working on Jim Leathers by the time Marquita returned. Jim Leathers lay perfectly still; only his eyes seemed alive. Those gray, hard eyes watched them while they examined him, but he made no attempt to speak.

"How's she feeling?" Bill Roper asked Marquita without looking up.

"The Gordon girl? She's all right. She went out to look over the horses or something."

"The Cheyenne Indians have a special way of doctoring a chest wound," Bob Stokes offered. "They catch as many red ants as they can get hold of, and they shove as many as they can in the wound and eat the rest."

"That's a real helpful suggestion," Roper complimented him. "Won't black ants do instead of red? Because we haven't got any black ants, either. Pull yourself together, Bob."

Old Joe had tangled with Jim Leathers before and hated his guts. "We'll send to Texas for some," he croaked. "What the hell? He's got plenty of time."

Bob Stokes tossed over his shoulder to

Marquita, "Get some more hot water, you."

"Bob, you better go see nothing's happened to Jody."

"I'll go in a minute, soon as we're through here."

But Jody came in of her own accord, before that. She went straight to Old Joe.

"Are you terribly uncomfortable, Joe?"

"I feel great," Joe said with spirit. "I been hunting for a vacation for fifteen years, and this is my first excuse!"

"I'm sorry, Joe. You'll never know how sorry I am. I tangled things up pretty badly, I guess."

"You done wonderful," Joe told her. "You saved Bill's neck, all right. They had him hog-tied like a mosshorn, and the girl, too, when we busted in."

Jody shot Marquita a glance in which the only light was a faint contempt, but she did not comment.

"I'm riding back to Miles," she told Joe. "On the way, I'll send help back, and everything you'll need. And I'll see that you're moved in a spring wagon, soon as you feel like moving. I appreciate what you've done, Joe, more than I can ever tell you."

She stooped over swiftly and kissed his cheek before she turned to Rob Stokes. "Rob, you're staying here. I'll send someone to help you as quickly as I can. But if they're not here tonight, they'll come sometime tomorrow at the latest. Good luck to you. I'm leaving now." And she kissed Rob Stokes, too.

"Hey, look," Rob Stokes began. "You can't be riding off like this in the middle of the night!"

"It's coming daylight, fast. I'll be all right."

As the door closed behind her, Rob Stokes smothered an oath and started after her, but Roper stopped him. "You'll stay here."

"How come you're giving orders?" Stokes flared at him.

"I give orders wherever I am."

Outside, in the gray light that seemed colder than the air, Jody Gordon had mounted as Rill Roper came to her stirrup.

"You mustn't go yet," he told her gently. "These boys are fixed as comfortable as they can be. There's no hurry to get help. You'll be wanting some coffee, and I have to talk to you, Jody."

"I'm not interested in talking to you," Jody said without expression.

"Why, Jody—look here—"

"I got you into this," Jody said. "I got you into this because I was a fool. So I had to get you out. That's all over now. I don't want to talk to you, now, or any time."

Roper, deeply puzzled, studied her gravely. "Jody," he asked, "tell me just one thing. Why did you come looking for me at Fork Creek?"

Jody's voice broke abruptly under the pressure of an emotion he could not identify. "Because I was a fool, an unbelievable fool! Such a fool as I'll never be again . . ."

She whirled her horse sharply, so that its hoofs, breaking the crust, sent up a scurry of dry snow. Then she was gone, her retreat covered by the cabin as she swung toward the trail.

For a moment, Roper stood looking after her. Then he stepped inside.

"You'll stay here, Bob," he said. Nobody ever knew—Roper himself did not know—why men who took orders from nobody else automatically took orders from him. "I'll saddle and ride after her, see that she gets to Miles."

"Wait a minute," Old Joe said. "You got to wait a minute! There's something else you got to know."

"There's nothing else I need to know."

"For one thing, every peace officer in Miles is waiting to lay hands on you, and you can't go there."

"I was going to Miles anyway," Roper said. "I want to talk to Lew Gordon."

"Lew Gordon ain't in Miles!"

"Then where the devil is he? His daughter—"

"Somebody—Jim Leathers, I guess—sent a note to Lew Gordon that his daughter was all right but couldn't be sent home just yet. Nobody signed that note. But it was plain to be seen from it that some war party of Ben Thorpe's was holding her some place. So Lew Gordon—"

"How do you know all this?"

"I was pony-riding back and forwards with Lew Gordon's orders on how we should go about hunting for Jody, and I happened to be there when this note came in. Lew Gordon—well, you can imagine how Lew Gordon took it."

"He blew up," Roper suggested.

"Well, no—that was a funny thing. He didn't exactly blow up. He just sat quietly for a long time. Then he says, 'This is the last straw; this sure is the last straw.' And after a long time, he sets out to clean that big old Betsy gun."

"You mean that Lew Gordon is going on the warpath himself? Hunting for Jody?"

"He's going after it straighter than that. Everybody knows Ben Thorpe is at Sundance. Lew Gordon has gone to Sundance to tie into Ben Thorpe, and his old gun is hammering away at his side."

"He figures to fight Thorpe?"

"Bill, it sure as hell looks that way to me. What's strange about that? Thorpe has punished away at Lew Gordon all his life. He stole his cattle and killed his trail bosses and fought him in the market fit to break them both, and finally he kills Lew's partner, and still he keeps on." A dry twist of a smile appeared on Old Joe's leathery face. "I could have told Ben he'd better look out—someday he was liable to do something to make Lew mad."

"Joe," Bill Roper said, "Joe—Walk Lasham himself is with Ben Thorpe!"

"Well—I ain't surprised."

"But God almighty, Joe, if he walks into a fight with those two, all hell can't save him! He's as good as dead, the minute he walks in there!"

"That," said Old Joe, "is what I figured you ought to know."

CHAPTER THIRTY-ONE

It was very early; the sun was only just breaking over the winter-starved prairie, that Sunday morning, as Bill Roper splashed through the creek that runs by Sundance, and rode into the little town. Overhead, the sky was such a clear, crystalline blue as Bill Roper had not seen since he left Texas, and underfoot his tired pony was sinking fetlock deep in thawed mud. The mud itself was predicting a spring which Roper believed now he would never see.

Without sign from the rider, Roper's pony drew up before the Palace Hotel and Livery—a false-fronted building in a Street of false fronts—perhaps attracted by no more than the smell of stored hay.

With some difficulty, Bill Roper roused a sleepy and resentful individual upon whom the Missouri hills were written plain.

"Feed this pony and feed him well."

Casually, Roper strolled along the corral where stood the loose horses which were being boarded here. He was chewing a straw as he came back to the sleepy man who was now shaking down hay.

"I see you have a 9B horse there—a good one."

"Yeah?"

"I figure Lew Gordon rode that horse in?"

"And supposin' he did?"

"Where is he stopping?"

"How the hell should I know? This dump is good enough for his horse, but it ain't good enough for him. He went to sleep with some friend or something, out at the edge of town."

Roper produced his tobacco and papers and slowly made himself a cigarette.

"I'll take a room facing this street," he said.

"No, you won't."

"Why won't I?"

"Last night was Saturday night. Rooms all filled up."

At this point, the argument was interrupted in a curious way. A tall and haggard man, in strangely nondescript clothes that were obviously not the clothes of a rider, appeared from the street. "You boys coming to church?"

"Church?"

"I've built a little church at the end of this street, in the name of the Lord, so I can carry the word of the Lord in this outlandish place. At the time of the service, you will hear its bell . . ."

Roper remembered the ramshackle little hut to which the far-wandering preacher referred. He had seen it as he had ridden in—a pitiful edifice of crooked boards, with a little makeshift bell tower in which hung some lost bell that nobody else wanted.

Roper rummaged in his pocket and found a

silver dollar. “Take this. Take this, and God help your work, and get goin’ . . .”

“I don’t know whether he hurts business or helps it,” the sleepy stableman said as the fantastic figure ambled away.

Roper shrugged. “I’ll take a front room on the street,” he said again.

“They’re all—”

“I don’t care anything about that.”

In the end, because this man always commanded others, a last night’s drunk was carried out of a front room above the stable—the room which Roper wanted—and Roper sat at last with his heels caught in the windowsill, resting as he regarded the empty street.

That Ben Thorpe was here was known to every cattleman in the north country. Ben Thorpe had been here many weeks; it was to Thorpe that Bill Roper was to have been delivered, here, if a kid horse wrangler following Jody Gordon had not shot Jim Leathers down. But, by the fine, hard-ridden 9B horse which Lew Gordon had ridden in. Bill Roper knew that Gordon had not been here long. He judged that he had got here in time.

Lew Gordon would hardly rest from the saddle without making his rendezvous with Thorpe. Presently Lew Gordon, or Ben Thorpe—or both—would walk along this quiet street, under this clear blue sky, through this fresh atmosphere of spring that one of them was not to see again . . .

Bill Roper sat there a long time. Seven o'clock passed, and eight, and nine, while he smoked and waited. He watched an old Mexican woman emerge from one nondescript house front and take refuge in another. He watched a razor-back pig wander out into the mud of the street, and a cur Indian dog drive it away again. He watched the gaunt preacher at his unhopeful task of canvassing for strays who might be persuaded into the little church he had brought here before its time.

Ten o'clock passed, and ten-thirty.

Then, upon the quiet main street of Sundance, appeared a figure that he knew—the one he had been waiting for.

It seemed to Bill Roper that Lew Gordon walked like a younger man than Roper had remembered. Bill Roper knew Lew Gordon by the flash of silver in his short beard, by the old hat, curiously like Dusty King's, which Lew Gordon had never changed. But he had to look twice to be sure that this man with the springy stride and erect bearing was the Lew Gordon he had known.

When he was sure, Bill Roper stood up and stretched. He filled his lungs with air, and at last let it go again, with a *whoof* like that of a pony which knows that it has come to the end of the long trail.

He drew a last drag from his cigarette and strapped on the gunbelt, which he had laid aside.

Unhurriedly, he drew the iron from its leather three or four times to be sure that it was running free. Then, with a purely unconscious motion, he cocked his hat over one eye and went down into the street.

The drowsy Missourian was not in evidence as Roper walked through the stable; the raider took time to be sure that his hard-ridden pony was well cared for before he left the Palace Hotel and Livery. He believed he had plenty of time.

He knew that Lew Gordon had gone into the Red Dog Saloon, and he walked toward it now. He was keenly conscious of the squish of his boot heels in the mud—a sound he had always hated. But now that he believed he would never hear it again, it was dear to him, as dear to him as breathing, as dear as needed food. All the blue sky, and all the gaunt prairie, melting out from under the winter snow, and the wet breeze from the spaces, and the sunlight itself—all these were incredibly precious to him, now that he believed he had come to the end. He drew deep breaths of that air that was both crisp and wet, and, turning his eyes to the blinding smash of the young sun itself, he knew that he did not want to die.

Down at the end of the street, where stood the ramshackle church with its crazy little steeple, half a dozen pigeons circled—symbols of a homely peace that Roper had never known. For a moment, Bill Roper, raider, night-rider, gunfighter—dreaded name of the Long Trail—experienced a twist of the heart, terrible, unbelievably acute. Then he shrugged and walked into the Red Dog Bar.

Lew Gordon stood at the bar of the Red Dog Saloon. The hard line of his jaw was blurred by a silver shag of whisker now, and his mustache was silver, and his hair, but the clear blue eyes were unbelievably young, younger than Bill Roper had ever seen them before. His hands were folded quietly, one elbow on the bar, and so greatly did this silver-haired man dominate the space in which he stood that it was minutes before Roper realized that there was a bartender there at all.

"So you came," Lew Gordon said.

"Of course, Lew. Didn't you know I would come?"

"In one way," Lew Gordon said, "I'm glad you came. I want to say a couple of things to you, Billy, my boy."

"Thorpe," Bill Roper said—"Is Thorpe coming here?"

"I sent for him," Gordon said. "Oh, yes, he'll come."

"How many with him?" Bill Roper said sharply.

"Do you care much, Billy?"

"No, Lew, I don't care."

"I done something wrong, Billy," Lew Gordon said. "You was right, and I was wrong. You fought him; I tried to smooth things out. I'm glad

I've lived to tell you this: You was right, and I was wrong!"

"Lew—" Bill began.

"I should have killed him, Billy," Lew Gordon said. It was strange how young Lew Gordon's eyes could look, clear and blue under silver bronze. "I should have killed him, Billy, long ago—when I first knew he killed your Dad . . ."

A thrust like the vitality of the prairie itself came up into Bill Roper, who thought he had resigned himself to death.

"Lew! What are you telling me?"

"Dusty knew," Lew Gordon said. "Dry Camp Pierce knows; I don't think anybody else does. You remember a pinto horse, Billy? By the pinto horse, we knew it was Ben Thorpe killed your father, on the Old Sedalia Trail—"

"All these years," Bill Roper said, "all these years you've known that, and you let this man live—"

"I know I was wrong." Lew Gordon said. Yet, somehow, he did not seem unhappy. "Always I stood for law, for order—the decent thing, the thing that would build this country into something my kid could live in. But—I guess it wasn't meant to be. I should have swung with you when you tied into him in Texas, and again when you tied into him in the north! But I aim to square it all up today!"

"You mean—?" said Bill Roper.

"He's coming to meet me here."

"With how many men?" Roper asked again.

"What does it matter?" Lew poured himself a drink.

Outside, on the boardwalk of Sundance, sounded the heels of approaching men . . .

"To your Dad," Lew Gordon said, "and in apology to you." Roper, who had ridden with Tex Long and Dave Shannon, had never seen a lighter or more carefree fight than shone then in the eyes of Lew Gordon, under those swiftly silvered brows.

"I can kill him," Bill Roper said, "I can kill him even if I die."

Lew Gordon's face changed swiftly. Suddenly, he was the indomitable old man whom Bill Roper had always known.

"Ben Thorpe is for me," he said.

"How can you figure that, when he killed my Dad—"

"This is for me," Lew Gordon said again, "to make up for the quiet years . . ."

And Bill Roper, looking deep into the young eyes of that aging man, finally said, "Okay."

The bartender said suddenly, nervously loud, "You gents want the same?"

It was as if neither of them had noticed him before. They saw him now, bald-headed, soft with standing, broken out of his sleepiness by a situation which he did not understand.

"The same," Lew Gordon said.

And then the door darkened, and the approaching heels on the boardwalk were silent because they had arrived. The man Lew Gordon had sent for had come . . .

It was Ben Thorpe who stepped quickly through the door, and one pace to the left, so that his gun, already drawn, swept the bar. It was Walk Lasham who followed him through the door, stepping one pace to the right, so that the door was clear for the three unknown gunfighters who tried to enter all at once.

Walk Lasham, dark, lean, and dour, with his strain of Indian blood showing strongly in his gaunt face, stood with his wide shoulders bowed in a suggestion of a crouch. Ben Thorpe, whom Bill Roper had not seen since the death of Dusty King, looked just as Roper remembered him to look . . . a hundred nights, in restless dreams, he had seen that big square-set frame, the big and mask-like face with its saddle-leathered skin, the unreadable but faintly malevolent stare of the heavy-lidded eyes. Thorpe looked a little older now, a little heavier than Roper remembered, but that was all.

"Draw, Ben," Lew Gordon said, and then all guns spoke at once.

In the blast of gunfire that followed, no man could tell what happened—but Roper knew that all guns seemed to converge upon Lew Gordon, and frantically he threw the lash of his fire at Thorpe, at Lasham, at the unknown men at the door.

For a moment, the guns spoke in a smashing roar, and the powder smoke stung Bill Roper's nostrils. Then suddenly, there was silence again, after the manner of gunfire, which begins abruptly with a lash of savage destruction, and ends again abruptly, in the same way.

Thorpe and Lasham both were down as that gunsmoke cleared, and those other strangers in the doorway had disappeared, except for a boot heel that dragged almost out of sight and then was still.

Beside the bar of the Red Dog Saloon, Lew Gordon still stood. Perhaps it was his bullet in the heart of Ben Thorpe—no man would ever know.

He turned now, slowly, elbow upon the bar, and looked at Bill Roper.

"Thanks, son," he said. The hand that held the heavy forty-five sagged deliberately, then dropped the gun, which made a strange clatter upon the unswept boards of the floor. Then Lew Gordon's knees buckled and he went down, and Bill Roper caught him as he fell.

Thin and tinny across the squalid town, across the thawing prairie, the church bell was ringing—a makeshift church bell ringing, on Sunday morning, as Lew Gordon died.

CHAPTER THIRTY-TWO

They buried Lew Gordon at Miles City. That dot upon the northern prairie marked, in effect, the farthest north reached by that great and dramatic upthrust of power which had welled up out of Texas, carving new trails, opening new vast countries, driving herds unnumbered, under the name of King-Gordon. Jody thought that her father would have wanted to lie there.

After that was done, Jody went back to Ogallala.

All through the spring, news kept trickling in. A swift bankruptcy was sweeping through Thorpe's loosely grouped organizations. Wiped out of Texas by the so-called Rustlers' War, broken in the north by the Great Raid—the shaken power of Ben Thorpe crumbled fast, now that Thorpe himself was dead. A once unbeatable organization, powerful from border to border, was going down in such utter debacle as no man could check.

And as Thorpe's power vanished into the gunsmoke in which he had died, a strange new prestige began to attach itself to the name of the man who had destroyed him. Only a little while ago, Bill Roper had been an outlaw, a hunted man with a price on his head, in whose behalf few men ever dared speak a good word. But now that his enemies were down, it seemed that the whole length of the Long Trail held men who professed themselves his lifelong friends. Like coyotes after a killing, like worms after rain, Bill Roper partisans were rising up, a score here, a hundred there, where not one friend had been, during those smoky hours of his greatest need. Already, men were less ready to remember what weapons he had used in fighting fire with fire than to remember simply that he had won. Three governors had issued blanket pardons for what he might or might not have done. He could have had almost any position he wanted near the top of any one of three or four of the great cattle companies. He could have had almost anything he wanted, then.

But Bill Roper—where was he? Nobody seemed to know. His own raiders—Tex Long, Hat Crick Tommy, Dave Shannon—now swaggering wherever they pleased amid a curious acclaim, did not know. And if Dry Camp Pierce, that one most trusted of all Bill Roper's men, knew where his leader was, he held his tongue.

Jody Gordon was making every effort to find out Bill Roper's whereabouts, and she had other than personal reasons for that. For, with the death of Lew Gordon, it suddenly appeared that Dusty King's share of King-Gordon was no longer to be withheld from the boy Dusty King had raised.

By Lew Gordon's will, King-Gordon was now divided in ownership between Jody Gordon and Bill Roper himself, this same Bill Roper upon whose head King-Gordon had such a little while ago placed a tempting price! A length of red tape longer than the Long Trail itself needed to be gone through before that split legacy could be straightened out, and everywhere in the West, Jody Gordon's men sought some word of Roper—without any success.

It was known that he had ridden out of Sundance, but after that, no one seemed to have seen him again. There was a rumor current now that he had been desperately wounded in the gunfight at the Red Dog Bar, and that somewhere, at some unknown and unmarked place upon the prairie, Bill Roper was dead.

The weeks passed, and the new grass came on the prairie, and still there was no word. Two or three times a week, after the first spring flowers began to show, Jody Gordon rode out to the pile of stone with its wooden cross that marked Dusty King's grave, putting there little handfuls of blue Indian hyacinth and white anemone.

And then suddenly one day, as she sat her horse before Dusty King's cross, she knew that Bill Roper was alive, that he was near, that he had come. The notch that she had seen Bill Roper cut in the arm of Dusty's cross to mark the death of Cleve Tanner was well weathered by this time, but now, sharp and freshly cut in the opposite arm of the cross, was a second notch that had never been there before.

A choking lump rose instantaneously in Jody's throat, and she spun her pony in its tracks as instinctively her eyes swept the plain and the low hills. So freshly cut was the new notch upon the cross that it seemed Bill Roper must still be no more than a few minutes away.

In the clear light of the late afternoon, she could make out every detail of the rambling little town of Ogallala, and the tower upon the house her father had built stood tall and clean, catching the sun, but nowhere was there to be seen any horseman. She turned her pony and rode home with a strange, empty, gone feeling, because for a moment Bill Roper had seemed so near and now was nowhere in sight.

When she had unsaddled, she went into the tall white house by the back way and walked through it slowly, preoccupied, wondering what she should do.

Then, as she came into the front room, her hand jumped to her throat, for someone was waiting for her there—a woman who stood up as Jody came in.

For a moment, Jody Gordon hardly recognized Marquita. This was partly because the westering sun was making a red blaze on the curtains behind her visitor, and Jody's eyes were not yet accustomed to the dimness within. But also because Marquita herself had changed. Marquita's black hair was drawn back from her face, very smooth and polished-looking, which made her face look thinner and sharper than Jody Gordon remembered. Only a little time had passed since they had faced each other in a remote cabin set in Montana snow, yet Marquita looked unmistakably older, and the live, sultry fire behind her dark slanting eyes was gone.

"I didn't realize," Jody said, "that you were in Ogallala."

"No, of course. I just came."

"To see me?"

"No. I'd hardly come to the sand hills for that, would I?" Jody noticed again the odd contrast between the soft, below-Rio-Grande speech and the direct American words. "I came to Ogallala because Bill Roper came."

"I see," Jody said without expression.

"No," Marquita said queerly, "you don't see. You can't possibly see. I guess that's why I'm here."

There was a little silence then, and Jody Gordon waited. Even if she had thought about it, she perhaps would not have felt it necessary to ask this woman to sit down, but Jody was not thinking about that.

"I lied to you," Marquita said. "I'm not sorry for that. I'd lie to you again, for the same reason, or for less reason. But this time it didn't do any good. So I thought I might as well tell you, since I was here."

"You lied to me?"

"I told you I was Bill Roper's girl. You naturally thought I was at Walk Lasham's camp because Bill Roper was there." Marquita's voice sounded curiously metallic and old, without that sultry fire to back it up. "Well, that wasn't so."

"You mean—you mean to say—"

"You don't understand much about men," Marquita said. Suddenly, for no reason, she seemed to be on the defensive. "You don't know what it is to love a man."

Jody Gordon heard herself say, "You think I don't?"

"Do you?"

"I love him," Jody said. Her voice was quiet, but her words were startling to herself. "I love him with all my heart, and all my body, and all my soul. There can't ever be any other man for me."

"Even if he belonged to me?"

"Even if he belonged to you, or to everybody, but me."

"Well," Marquita said, "he did not belong to me, not even for one minute, in all my life. How do you think you would like that, in my place?"

"But—at the Lasham camp you said—"

"I know I did. I would have got him if I could,

in any way I could. I even came here because I knew he was coming here. But now I can just as well tell you it's hopeless, and I'm through. After all, I don't need to run after any man, not anymore."

"You mean—you're willing to let him go—even if—"

"Let him go? I never had him." An odd edge of contempt came into Marquita's voice, but whether for Jody or herself was not plain. "Can't you get that through your head?" She turned toward the door impatiently. Perhaps she could not remember why she had come to a meeting for which she now found nothing but distaste. "I tell you I don't need your man, or any man. Ben Thorpe died broke but Walk Lasham didn't; he was too clever for that. Walk Lasham left everything he had to me—it was Walk Lasham who was my man. I can go back to my own people now. Don't fret yourself—I haven't anything to worry about anymore."

Jody said curiously, "Why did you come to me?"

"I haven't the least idea why I came." Marquita's hand was on the door latch now. "Maybe it was because I feel sorry for you. I feel sorry for you, because you are a little fool."

Jody Gordon supposed that she ought to thank Marquita for having come here, for having made the confession which she had made, but she was confused, and the words would not come. Instead, she said, "Do you know where he is? Is he well? Is he safe and all right?"

Marquita's smile was mocking. "You want me to find him and send him to you?"

"I think," Jody said, "he'll come."

"Okay," Marquita said, and she pulled open the door.

It was still impossible for Jody Gordon to understand Marquita; she could not understand the guiding lines of Marquita's life, nor the moods and emotions that had pressed Marquita to choose them. Most of the episodes of Marquita's stormy career would probably have been unimaginable to Jody. Yet now Jody recognized in Marquita a certain strain of wild, hawk-like gallantry.

"I want to tell you something," Jody said. "I want to tell you I appreciate—your letting me know—"

Marquita flashed a queer hard smile; there was bitterness in it, more bitterness in her smile than in her words. "Keep your thanks to yourself." Then she was gone.

After a moment, Jody heard the hoofs of a team, and the wheels of the carriage in which Marquita had come—and gone—slicing the deep mud . . .

Yet, Bill Roper did not come.

When two days had passed, a panic caught

Jody Gordon, and she began to haunt the vicinity of Dusty King's cross, out on the prairie beside the trail over which Dusty King, with Bill Roper beside him, had brought those first weary herds of cattle in. She believed that Roper would not leave the Ogallala country without visiting once more the grave of Dusty King, for whose death he had fought the Texas Rustlers' War, and conceived Montana's Great Raid, and brought down Ben Thorpe himself in the end.

But it was the evening of the fourth day, before Roper came.

CHAPTER THIRTY-THREE

Sitting her quiet pony beside Dusty King's pile of stone, Jody Gordon saw Roper riding toward her when he was still a long way off. Roper was not alone. Beside him rode a little grasshoppery figure in disreputable clothes, which Jody recognized as that of Dry Camp Pierce. Somehow, Dry Camp had managed to rejoin his chief when the others could not. It was typical of Dry Camp that he was riding beside Bill Roper now, would always be typical, so long as both of them should live.

The two riders hesitated at the five hundred yards. Roper said something to Dry Camp Pierce, and after a moment or two, Dry Camp turned his horse and went back. Bill Roper came on alone. Perhaps he feared this meeting more than anything he had ridden into yet—but she knew he would not turn.

It seemed to Jody Gordon that time lagged forever as Billy Roper's pony slowly approached, and it seemed to her that that slow approach was characteristic of all that had happened to them—delay, and delay, while wars were fought, and raids struck in, all through those smoky years in which they had been apart.

And yet, at last, when he stopped his horse

beside her, and they looked at each other, there was something between them still, as if the smoky years themselves had built a wall.

Bill Roper said, “Hello, Jody. You’re looking mighty well.”

Jody said, “I’m all right.”

There was a pause, curiously awkward. In the pause, Jody’s horse struck at the cinch with a hind foot, tormented by an early fly.

“You didn’t come to see me,” Jody said.

“Well,” Bill Roper said slowly—“I didn’t know if you’d want me to.”

“Don’t you know that you’re half of King-Gordon? And I’m the other half.”

“Jody—people like you and me can’t go by things like that—things like legacies and wills.”

Jody’s voice was very quiet, yet it must have seemed to Bill Roper that she cried out. “You’re going to leave me to carry all this, just by myself?”

“Lew Gordon left a sound organization,” Bill Roper said, his voice dead. “You have many men, and good men, too. The works will roll, I think, with Thorpe gone.”

Once more, the long, strangely poignant silence. And to Jody, it seemed a terrible thing that what they both wanted was the same thing, and that yet the smoky years somehow managed to stand between.

Jody Gordon turned away from Bill Roper and faced Dusty King's cross. She sat her saddle very straight before that cross, clean-limbed and slender, and there was something in her face that was enduring. It was the face of a woman who turned to the future without a trace of doubt or fear. And she was the loveliest thing that Bill Roper would ever see . . .

"Jody," Bill Roper said uncertainly, "I want to tell you something. Other men will have to fight other wars, but my part of all that is finished. I'm not sorry my gun is hung up. I hope it's hung up forever. Once I thought that when Thorpe was smashed, my work would be through—but now I see it's only begun. I think we're going to build something pretty fine, if you'll stay by me."

Jody smiled a little. Without taking her eyes from the cross, she reached her hand toward him and took his.

"All the anger and the hate has gone out of me," Roper said, "and if you can only someday understand that my riding with the wild bunch was—was what I had to do—"

He fumbled for words and stopped.

"Give me your knife," Jody said.

"My—my what?"

She turned, and herself drew his skinning knife from the sheath at his belt. Then she stepped to the ground.

“In justice,” Jody said, “in justice, and in memory of courage.”

With her own hands, she cut the third notch upon the cross, deep and clean.

ABOUT THE AUTHOR

Alan LeMay began writing at the age of sixteen, and, he said, "thereafter spent a great many years trying to escape. By 1935, I was able to stock a cattle ranch of sufficient size to engage most of my time, thus following in the footsteps of my grandfather, who was an early Kansas cattleman. No, I guess I was following more in the footsteps of my other grandfather, who was killed by a buffalo on the Solomon River, for the following year I bet it would rain, overloading my range to the limit of my resources. I was right to an amazing degree. It rained so hard the feed washed out, and I went broke to the extent of my credit, which was excellent."

He eventually gave up and became a writer after all. LeMay wrote countless magazine stories and many mystery and western novels, as well as screenplays for Hollywood.

He is best remembered for his two classic Western novels, *The Searchers* (1954) and *The Unforgiven* (1957), both of which were adapted into the motion pictures: *The Searchers* (1956), starring John Wayne, Jeffrey Hunter, and Natalie Wood, and directed by John Ford, which was named The Greatest Western Movie of All Time by the American Film Institute in 2008, and *The*

Unforgiven (1960), starring Audrey Hepburn and Burt Lancaster, and directed by John Huston. LeMay wrote and directed *High Lonesome* (1950), starring John Drew Barrymore and Chill Wills, and featuring Jack Elam.

LeMay was the author of eighteen novels and dozens of short stories, later published in five different collections: *Spanish Crossing* (1998); *The Bells of San Juan* (2001); *West of Nowhere* (2002); *Painted Rock* (2004); and *Tonopah Range: Western Stories* (2006).

Center Point Large Print
600 Brooks Road / PO Box 1
Thorndike, ME 04986-0001 USA

(207) 568-3717

US & Canada:
1 800 929-9108
www.centerpointlargeprint.com